$6.99

TOUGH CALL!

Roberto "Magic" Ramirez was hot.

On the mound at the top of the seventh, Magic glanced over to the scoreboard. For the opposing team from Boston, nothing but zeroes in every column.

Suddenly, the announcement blasted over the PA: "Now batting for Boston: David Green!"

Magic snapped to attention. His best friend. And the most awesome power hitter in the league. He tugged on his hat as Green stepped into the box and smiled.

Roberto got a signal for a fastball, and fired. The pitch came in wide.

"Hey, Ramirez! How about a *real* pitch!" Green yelled, and choked up on his bat.

The catcher looked over at the L.A. dugout, nodded, then called time and hustled out to the mound

"Bossman says to brush this hot dog back."

"Can't do that, man. I know the guy."

"Hey, kid, wake up," he said, handing Roberto the ball. "This ain't a high-school game."

Other books in the ROOKIES series:

Mark Freeman

Library of Congress Catalog Card Number: 90-92272

ISBN 0-345-35904-9

Printed in Canada

First Edition: June 1990

Special thanks to Tim Cockey.

RLI: $\dfrac{\text{VL: 6 \& up}}{\text{IL: 6 \& up}}$

Copyright © 1989 by the Jeffrey Weiss Group, Inc.

Produced by the Jeffrey Weiss Group, Inc.
133 Fifth Avenue
New York, New York 10003

Library of Congress Catalog Card Number: 89-90721

ISBN 0-345-35904-6

Printed in Canada

First Edition: July 1989
Seventh Printing: January 1995

This book is dedicated to John M. and Charlie C.
With special thanks, of course, to Wendy.

ONE

"Hey, kid. Think fast!"

David Green was in the clouds. Who wouldn't be on his first day of spring training? He couldn't believe it.

"Hey! Kid!"

Green blinked and turned his head just in time to see a ball about to hit him. Instinctively, he ducked, spearing out with his glove and nabbing the ball. The left fielder, who had tossed it, laughed. His name was Pete Kenney.

"Sorry, kid," Kenney said. "Did I interrupt your sleep?"

Green felt his face turning red.

"No. I mean . . . uh, no."

Kenney laughed again. "Oh, I see. Since you put it that way."

Still chuckling, Kenney trotted back over to his

position. Green turned the other way and fired the ball over to the right fielder. He slammed his fist into his glove. *Come on,* Green told himself, *this is the majors! You snooze, you lose. Heads up now!*

A strong breeze was blowing in from right field. A warm breeze; the warmest breeze David Green had ever felt in the middle of February, that's for sure. Back home in Rosemont, Illinois, Green's younger brothers were probably out shoveling snow this very minute. Green had talked to his mom on the phone last night. A big storm had blown in from Canada. Fifteen inches.

They had better *be shoveling snow,* Green thought. *With a little hustle, a guy can make some good money after a snowstorm.* And every little bit counted.

Ever since the old man had abandoned the family, Green's mom had done her best to raise the three girls and four boys by herself. And Green knew that it was sure no picnic. As the oldest, he had always done his part. But now that he was down in Florida trying to fight his way onto the team, Green would have to count on the others to pull their share back home. Green told himself that right after the game he'd call home just to make sure that everything was okay.

But boy . . . wouldn't they be jealous!

Green looked behind him. A row of tall palm trees ran along behind the home-run fence, their big leaves waving in the wind. The sun was high and beating down to the tune of eighty-five degrees. *Eighty-five degrees!* In February!

Man, Green thought, *I love the major leagues!*

Green took a toss from the right fielder and in a single motion, whipped the ball off to Pete Kenney, who caught it and tossed it in.

"Look alive now, Shorty!" Kenney called out. "Here comes the real thing!"

Green socked his glove a few times and bent forward. Shorty. Some joke. At six foot five, David Green was anything but a shorty. In fact, years ago a simple flip of a coin had steered Green away from pursuing a promising basketball career. Green was a natural athlete in every way. His coaches and teachers back at Rosemont High had never once doubted that he would be a big success in whatever he did. With his brown hair and blue eyes, and that all-American smile, Green was a natural charmer and easily the most popular guy at school. Things just came to him easily.

And as far as Green could tell, they still were. After all . . . here he was.

Green ran his free hand across the words stitched on his uniform. Red Sox. The Boston Red Sox! He still couldn't believe it.

Green wondered what his buddies were doing right now, right this minute. Over in Vero Beach, about two hours away, was Roberto Ramirez. Magic Ramirez. Magic had been drafted by the Dodgers. What a lucky break that the Dodgers trained in Florida. That meant there would be a few exhibition games between them and the Red Sox. Once the regular season started, of course, the Dodgers would be off in the National League, and the only way Magic and Green would meet up in a game then would be in the All-Star Game, or maybe the World . . .

He was getting ahead of himself. First, you've got to make the team.

The first batter was stepping in, rapping the bat against his cleats to get the dirt out. Green pounded his glove. Here goes nothing.

The pitcher let loose with a fastball. The batter squared around and laid down a perfect bunt that dribbled halfway to third base and then just stopped. By the time the third baseman even had his hands on the ball, the batter was standing safely at first.

Green couldn't believe it. A bunt! The lead-off man in his first at bat? In spring training? The crowd booed good-naturedly. It was a good trick.

Kenney was chuckling and shaking his head. He called out to Green. "Pretty smooth, eh?"

Green thought about his buddy, Glen Mitchell. Scrapper. That was just the sort of move Scrapper would've made, the surprise bunt. It was gutsy and clever. So was Scrapper. Scrapper had been drafted by the White Sox. In a lot of ways, Green figured, the pressure was probably the worst on old Scrap. After all, the White Sox was their home team, his and Scrap's and Magic's. Folks back home in Rosemont would be following Scrap Mitchell's every move. And that meant Scrapper's father, too, Joe Mitchell, the former Philadelphia Phillies star. And Green knew all too well what Scrapper thought about *that*. Not much.

The next batter came up and hit a high fly ball to left, which Kenney caught easily. He threw the ball back in to the infield and held up one finger.

"One down!"

Green squinted in toward the plate. He knew that the next batter had a great swing. The outfield coach was sweeping his arms to the right. He wanted the outfielders to shift. Green started to jog to his right.

"Yo, Green!" Kenney called out. "Be cool now. Just stroll on over. Don't give him any ideas."

The left fielder was strutting along like the original Mr. Cool. Green turned red again. The only thing worse than being a rookie is acting like a rookie. He stopped jogging and took a few more steps to the right. Real casual.

Kenney called out, "Yeah! You got it."

Green shrugged and called back, "Hey, I'm not out here to strut around. I'm here to play ball."

Kenney thought this was funny.

"Serious business, eh, Shorty?"

Green spit into his glove. "You bet."

The count went to two and two, and then the batter laced a clean single into shallow right. Green rushed over to back up the right fielder, who took the ball on one bounce. The lead runner held up at second. Green trotted back to his position.

"Good hustle," the left fielder called out.

Green didn't answer. *I'll show you good hustle,* he thought. *Just give me a good chance.*

The next batter played cat and mouse with the pitcher, fouling off pitch after pitch, before finally slicing at a curve ball that wasn't there.

Two on, two out.

As the next batter came up, Kenney called out, "Watch out for this one!"

But he didn't really have to. It was the opposing team's catcher. And Green knew the book on him. Very simple: big bat. This guy wouldn't be sneaking a bunt. No way. He'd be aiming for those palm trees standing there behind the outfield fence.

Green took a few steps back. He checked the pennants that were flapping over the top of the grandstand. If the ball got up into that wind . . . kiss her good-bye.

As the pitcher went into his windup, Green leaned forward and went up on his toes. He licked his lips. His ears were buzzing. This one could be his.

Crack!

The crowd was on its feet. Green hadn't even seen the pitch, but he knew immediately that the ball was headed his way! Instinctively, Green started to backpedal even before he had seen the ball. Green looked up and spotted the ball already almost directly over his head. It was up in that wind and sailing back toward the fence. He turned. But his feet tangled, and he dropped to one knee.

His first shot in the majors, and he had screwed up!

The crowd was roaring like one big machine as the ball sailed toward the fence. But Green didn't even hear them. It was now or never. He pushed himself off the grass like a sprinter coming out of the blocks. His cleats ripped at the grass. Green did something he knew he should never do. Never.

If Coach La Russo, his old high-school coach, had seen him do it, he would have chewed him out for an hour.

He took his eye off the ball.

Green lowered his head and dug as hard as he had ever dug in his life, right for the fence. The ball was already beginning to come down now. There was no way . . . Pete Kenney had already slowed to a trot, figuring this ball was history.

And then suddenly, a locomotive came by, dressed as a baseball player. Head down, Green came running full tilt! The ball was dropping fast, a good ten feet to his left.

Kenney couldn't believe it. "What the . . ."

Green leaped. Pete Kenney would say later that the rookie flew. The ball and Green and the fence all came together at once. Green crashed into the fence, came down on the black gravel of the warning track, and skidded right up to Kenney's feet, tumbling over and over like a can that someone has kicked along a sidewalk.

The crowd went silent. The only sound was the guy who had laced the ball, huffing and puffing around third, positive of his home run. The second-base umpire was trotting out toward Green. Green rolled onto his back and saw Kenney staring down at him.

"Man, are you crazy!" Kenney said.

And then Green held up his glove. He had the ball!

"Out!" the umpire yelled. The crowd went crazy. The batter skidded to a stop halfway between third and home. *He* went crazy.

"He got it?"

No one could remember ever seeing such an incredible catch. Who was this kid? The coaches for the opposing team were riffling through their report books.

Green and the left fielder jogged in together. Kenney was all grins, pounding Green on the back.

"I don't believe it," he kept saying. "Great catch, kid."

Green felt great. If only Magic and Scrapper could have seen it. His first major-league catch! The most sensational of his career! The other players were coming off the bench to congratulate him. The left fielder was still pounding his back as the mob hit.

"Shorty, if you can hit like you can catch . . ."

Green turned to him and broke into a big grin. "You ain't seen nothing yet!"

Coach Brooks, the Red Sox's batting coach, was standing nearby in the dugout. When he overheard the remark, he frowned and followed the rookie over to the water cooler.

"Nice grab, Green," the coach said, though he didn't sound too enthusiastic.

Green downed a cup of water, then tossed the cup aside.

"Piece of cake," he said. And then he joked, "I do that with my eyes closed."

Brooks looked at him closely.

"With your eyes closed, huh? That's how you plan to make the team? With your eyes closed?"

Green laughed. "Well, you know what I mean."

Brooks leaned past him and got a cup of water.

He drank it down, then tossed the paper cup down next to Green's.

"Not really, kid," Brooks said. "Maybe you'll show me."

Green got his chance a few innings later. The manager had stuck him in the number-seven slot on the lineup. Green chuckled at that. He *always* batted cleanup. Oh well, they'd learn.

Green forgot, until he stepped into the batter's box, that it was the opposing team's catcher whose hit Green had snared.

"Well, look who it is," the catcher grumbled. "Superman."

Green knew that the guy was trying to psych him out. He was a veteran, after all. A real-life big leaguer. But Green remembered what he and Scrap and Magic had told each other at the airport in Chicago before flying down here. "Don't let them intimidate us. We're here because we're good. And we'll get into the majors because we're great!"

Green rapped against his cleats with the bat and looked the catcher square in the eye.

"It's not Superman," he said. "It's DT. 'Downtown' to you."

He couldn't believe he had said it. Sure, that was his nickname back in high school. And it had stuck with him last year in the minors. But this was different. You don't go around talking like that to major leaguers. Unless you're ready to back it up.

The catcher chuckled. "Downtown, eh? You

mean like, over the fence? Like where my hit was supposed to go?"

Green didn't answer. He dug in and waited for the pitch. It came in, just at the letters.

"Strike!"

Green stepped out of the box. *What's wrong?* he asked himself. *That was my pitch. That's the one I always cream. I probably won't see it again for a month.*

The second pitch came in high and outside. Green swung and missed. The catcher tossed the ball back to the pitcher.

"Downtown, eh?" he said. "Looks more like 'downwind.'"

Green ignored him. The pitcher tried to finesse the next two pitches. They were both wide, and Green didn't take the bait. The pitcher shook off the next few signs, then seemed to get one he liked. The catcher shifted, and held up his glove.

"So long, Downwind" he murmured.

The pitch came in. It was a sinker, but it was hanging just a little. Green dropped his shoulder and stepped into it.

Crack!

The ball flew up into the blue Florida sky. Green knew right away it was gone. Home run.

He turned to the catcher and tipped his cap. "So long, mister."

Green rounded the bases at a fast trot. Coach Brooks had come out on the dugout steps to watch. But he wasn't smiling like the rest of the team. He was just watching. As Green rounded third, he saw the coach standing there and he saw the look on his face. On impulse, Green flashed the coach the thumbs-up. Brooks frowned even more.

The catcher was standing at the plate as Green came in. He was holding his mask in his hand and shaking his head slowly. Green smiled at him as he touched the plate.

The guys in the dugout were cheering as he trotted over. So was the crowd. Green pulled off his cap and waved it at the crowd. They ate it up. Green looked up at the pennants flapping over the grandstand.

It might be cold in Chicago, he thought to himself. *But in Florida, it's hot!*

TWO

Roberto "Magic" Ramirez knew it was silly, but for him it was true. Whenever anyone said good luck to him before he pitched a game, it turned out to be bad luck. It was silly, but that's just the way it was. And Magic Ramirez wasn't the sort of guy to mess around with the way things were.

Magic was about to pitch in his first spring-training game for the Dodgers. It was only an exhibition game, and Magic was only going to pitch the first three innings. Even if he was brilliant, the pitching coach had told him that he would be pulled after the three innings.

"We need to take a look at everyone," the coach said. And then he added, "But, hey, good luck."

Magic paced up and down the long corridor between the clubhouse and the dugout. *Don't think*, he told himself, *just do it*. But Magic

Ramirez couldn't help but think. That's how he was. As he paced up and down the corridor trying to calm himself, he wondered about being a doctor. If he hadn't gone into baseball, he'd be in school instead of in the dugout, worrying about exams. Maybe it was true what his friends had said about him. Maybe he was just born to worry.

Magic had read in the paper that morning about David's great catch and his home run over in Winter Haven. Green was off to a good start. *He'll make it*, Magic thought. The all-American boy with the dynamite bat. *He'll make it. And so will Scrapper. Good old Scrap. He'll make it on guts alone, if he has to.*

But Magic was not so sure about himself. He knew he was good, of course. He had the best split-fingered fastball around. With it he had smashed every pitching record in Rosemont High history, and then had gone on to do just about the same last year on the Dodgers' farm team. And he knew that when he was in the groove with the rest of his pitches, he was practically unstoppable.

When he was in the groove.

"Hey, Ramirez! Let's go!"

Magic trotted down to the dugout and out to the mound. He tossed a few more warm-up pitches. He felt loose. He felt good. Magic knew that he was in excellent physical condition. All winter he had worked out with weights and jogged along the banks of Lake Michigan every day. Magic ran like a boxer, pumping his fists in the air. Some people even said that he looked a little like Rocky, with his dark, curly hair and brown eyes. Magic was a lean six foot one. Coach La Russo used to call him the "lean, mean, pitching machine."

The pitching machine kicked at the dirt around the rubber, then looked around the park. It was a pretty decent crowd for a spring-training game. But then, why not? This wasn't just the Dodgers playing; this was the Dodgers versus the Yankees. Champs versus champs.

Magic glanced toward the Yankee dugout. There they were, in their famous pinstripes. These were guys that Magic used to watch on TV. And now here they were, in person! And he was throwing against them! It was too much.

Magic gulped. *Just stay loose*, he told himself. *Just get that first pitch off. Give him your best.*

The catcher, Tommy Pearson, jogged out to the mound.

"Okay, kid. I've been fishing all winter, and I'm a little rusty, so nothing fancy right up front, right? Fastball. Curve. Slider. In and out. The basics."

Magic nodded his head. His throat was too dry to speak.

Pearson handed him the ball. "Okay, then. Good luck."

Good luck? Magic took a deep breath.

The first batter up was Robby Hendrix. Great. Only one of the consistently best hitters on the Yankees in the last ten years. Hendrix dug in and took a few practice swings. The catcher signaled for a fastball on the inside corner. Magic got a good grip on the ball. *Here goes.*

For a split second, he saw his whole life flash before his eyes. He let loose with one of the hardest pitches he had ever thrown. The force of his follow-through almost threw him to the ground. He knew it would be a strike.

Hendrix swung. And connected. Magic couldn't believe it. He was positive that he had never seen a ball hit as hard as that one. He turned and watched the ball sailing higher and higher, zooming down the left-field line and heading right out of the park. The outfielders hadn't even moved. They just stood there with their hands to their sides and watched the comet fly.

But the ball went foul. It bounced off into the parking lot over four hundred and fifty feet away. When Magic looked back toward the plate, Hendrix was spitting into his hands and getting a good grip on the bat.

"Okay," Hendrix called out. "I'm ready now!"

Magic stepped down off the mound and picked up the rosin bag. He had just seen the fastest pitch of his life lifted right out of the park. He glanced back at Hendrix, who was standing there, casually swinging his bat. It suddenly looked as big as a tree.

What do I do next? Magic asked himself. *He's going to murder anything else I put up there.* Already, he saw his whole career going straight down the drain.

Pearson trotted out to the mound.

"Hey, don't sweat it. That's just Robby's way of saying hello."

"Yeah," said Magic. "Right."

The pitching coach came out of the dugout, calling, "Time!" to the umpire. This was Coach

McGreevey, the guy who had made the final decision to bring Ramirez up from the minors. *Oh great*, Magic said to himself. *He's coming out to yank me. So much for the majors.*

"What's wrong, Ramirez?" McGreevey said when he reached the mound. "You've never seen a foul ball before?"

"Not like that," Magic answered.

The coach and the catcher exchanged a quick look. The catcher shrugged.

"Look," McGreevey said to Ramirez. "Don't mess around with this guy. Give him your split-fingered fastball."

The catcher shook his head. "But that pitch acts like a sinker, Coach. It breaks right down where Hendrix loves 'em."

Coach McGreevey winked at Magic.

"I've seen that pitch. Believe me, he won't love it."

Pearson shook his head. "He'll cream it. I'll bet you a steak dinner."

McGreevey grinned at this. "I'll go make the reservations."

The coach headed back to the dugout. The catcher smiled and dropped the ball into Magic's glove.

"It's his money."

He went back and took up his position behind the plate. He beat against his glove, then held it up.

"Come on, kid. Bring it in!"

Magic felt for the stitches on the ball. *Here goes nothing*, he thought. Magic wound and threw. The ball sailed right for the strike zone. Hendrix swung, but the ball dipped just under his bat at the last instant.

"Strike two!"

Pearson couldn't believe it. Coach McGreevey yelled something from the dugout which Magic couldn't hear. But he was pretty sure it had something to do with steak.

"Giving the boy a little breeze, Robby?" the catcher chuckled.

Hendrix dug in. He didn't see what was so funny. The catcher called again for the split-finger fastball. *No*, Magic thought. *He's onto it.* But the catcher wouldn't let him shake it off. Coach McGreevey was up on the top step of the dugout, watching closely.

Magic set for the pitch. He cranked and fired. Hendrix was still swinging as the ball pounded into the catcher's glove.

"Strike three! Yer out!"

He had done it! He had struck out Robby Hendrix on three straight pitches. Over in the dugout, Coach McGreevey was rubbing his stomach and licking his lips.

The next two batters came up and went down the same way. Magic had struck out the side. He had sent the Yankees down in order!

In the dugout, Coach McGreevey was ribbing the catcher.

"Yeah, I like 'em rare and I like 'em big. Sirloin."

A couple of the guys gave Magic the thumbs-up.

"Nice pitching, kid."

"You had him talking to himself."

Tommy Lasorda, the Dodgers' manager, went over to Coach McGreevey.

"Next inning, put a gun on the kid. I want to see how fast that ball is going."

Magic sat down on the bench, trying to keep the hugest smile in the world from showing on his face. The catcher pulled off his glove and held up his hand for the others to see.

"Look at that," he joked. "Ramirez threw that ball so fast it took the lines right off my hand!"

The guys laughed.

Magic struck out two more batters in his three innings. The other batters all grounded out or flew out. It was three scoreless innings against the Yankees.

Back in the locker room, Magic pulled off his uniform shirt and hung it in the locker. Off in the showers, some guys were flipping each other with wet towels. Magic sat down to take off his cleats, but instead found himself just staring at the uniform. Dodgers.

He pinched himself. It wasn't a dream. It was real.

Magic couldn't even wait until he was back at the motel to call his family and tell them the good news. On his way back from the shower, he spotted a pay phone just past his locker. He grabbed some change and, standing in his towel, dripping wet, he dialed his number. Angelina, his older sister, answered the phone.

"You struck out the Yankees!" she screamed

into the phone when he told her the news. "Hey! Roberto knocked out the Yankees!"

Angelina put Magic's mother on the phone. She was so excited, all she could do was cry.

Magic's kid sister, Maria, got on next. Maria didn't really care that much about baseball one way or the other. But Magic thought she was pretty cool, anyway, for a sister. When he told Maria about his pitching debut, she only said, "Neat."

Neat. Typical.

Magic looked around and saw that the locker room was already almost empty. "Hey, Maria," he said. "Put Dad on."

When he heard his father's voice, Magic cleared his throat.

"Say, Dad, I just wanted to tell you that everything's fine down here. Hey, I struck out Robby Hendrix!"

"Is he good?" Carlos Ramirez asked.

"Good? He's the best! *Nobody* strikes out Robby Hendrix!"

Magic's dad let out a small laugh. "Well, it looks like somebody does now."

Magic felt great. He thanked his father for all the support he had given him.

"Look, Dad, if this, uh, if this doesn't work out, I want you to know that I could still get into a pre-med program. I mean, I socked away most of my bonus."

"It sounds to me like it is working out just fine," Carlos Ramirez answered. "We'll make the decision about school soon enough."

"Yeah, but if—"

"No, ifs. You do your best, son, and I will be proud of you."

As Magic was hanging up the phone, he heard his mother's voice in the background. *"Get plenty of sleep!"*

Magic chuckled. He thought again about Robby Hendrix going out on strikes. One. Two. Three! *If I get any sleep tonight*, Magic thought, *it'll be a miracle.*

THREE

If there was one thing Glen Mitchell knew, it was that he shouldn't be late for the first game of spring training. But he was. And it was his own fault. But what could he say? Sorry, Coach, but I was dreaming about being in the World Series and I slept late? Turning fantastic double plays and triple plays in your dreams is one thing, but Mitchell knew he would only be getting a few chances to prove that he could do it in the real thing. And now here he was, running late.

The team was already suited up when Mitchell arrived at the park. The first person he ran into was the White Sox manager, Coach Cunningham.

"That's a pretty interesting uniform you've got there, Mitchell."

Cunningham wasn't smiling. He was being sarcastic.

"Uh . . . sorry, Coach," Mitchell stammered.

Cunningham looked at him. "Oh, you're sorry, huh? Well, that's good of you to apologize, Mitchell. I'm sorry, too. I was sort of hoping we might get a look at you today. A lot of folks around here are curious to see how the son of Joe Mitchell stacks up."

Anger flashed through Mitchell. His father. Always his father. You would think that nobody else in the history of the world had ever played first base for the Philadelphia Phillies except Joe Mitchell. Sure, Mitchell thought, it was great that his dad was so famous. He was proud of his dad. He had even ridden with him in the parade that Philadelphia had in his honor the day he retired from baseball. But still, it was tough, always being compared with him.

"Do you think your father was ever late to a game?" Cunningham asked.

Mitchell knew that he had to keep his temper. He was already starting off on the wrong foot.

"I don't know, Coach," he said tensely. "I'll have to ask him."

Cunningham looked at him hard to see if he was being flip.

"They call you 'Scrapper,' don't they?" he said.

Scrapper nodded. "Yeah."

Cunningham nodded his head. He was about to say something else, but instead he said, "Okay, Mitchell, suit up. I've got a spot on the bench I need to keep warm."

Scrapper's face turned red as he went into the

empty locker room. *Boy*, he thought, *I really blew it.*

Scrapper changed quickly into his uniform. He used to joke with Green and Magic that he could get dressed faster than them because there was less of him to get dressed. Scrapper was five foot seven and 165 pounds. All muscle.

As he sat on the bench, watching the White Sox taking a pounding, he wished that Coach Cunningham would give him a chance. He realized that he was being punished for being late. He wondered if he was also being "punished" for being Joe Mitchell's son. That kind of thing had happened before.

The Sox were getting creamed. What a drag. Scrapper looked out of the dugout and saw Ted Leonard, the guy who did sports for ABC-TV in Chicago. Leonard saw Scrapper looking at him, and he waved. Leonard had interviewed Scrapper and the others a couple of times over the last few years. Scrapper waved back. Cunningham saw him do it.

"Are you swatting flies, Mitchell?"

"Uh, no, Coach."

The coach turned away. An idea came to Scrapper. *What the heck*, he thought. *I've got nothing to lose*. He cleared his throat.

"In fact, Coach, I'm not swatting anything, and I wish I was."

"Yeah?" Cunningham asked.

"I mean, I *could* be swatting runs if you'd put me out there."

A couple of other guys in the dugout groaned when they heard that. But Scrapper dove right in. He jumped to his feet.

"I mean it, Coach. I'm sorry about being late and everything. But I'm going nuts in here."

A couple of guys laughed.

Cunningham looked hard at Scrapper. *Uh-oh*, Scrapper thought. *Now I've done it. A good player doesn't beg, he just follows the manager's instructions.*

Coach Cunningham shrugged, then turned his head and looked back out toward the field as if he had completely forgotten that Scrapper Mitchell even existed. Scrapper sat back down and glared down the first guy who dared smile at him.

But about a batter later, Coach Cunningham said quietly, "Mitchell, you go in and play second in the next inning. Loosen up."

The White Sox were behind eight to nothing by the bottom of the fifth. It was a romp. The team just didn't seem to have any energy. They were swinging at air and running in mud.

Off on the sidelines stood Scrapper Mitchell, loosening up. Half the crowd was watching *him* instead of the game. The team had a couple of buckets of oranges for the players to eat for energy during the game. But Scrapper had pulled the buckets out of the dugout and he got two guys to start rolling the oranges at him as fast as they could. At first it was a funny sight, then it was impressive. As fast as the oranges came bounding up to him, Scrapper scooped them up and flipped them back, bare handed. Faster and faster. The crowd loved it.

Up in the stands, Ted Leonard was making notes.

The Sox went down in order. Scrapper grabbed his glove and ran out onto the field.

Because the Sox were already so far behind, the guys weren't putting out a lot of effort. But Scrapper knew only one way to play: a hundred and ten percent!

Scrapper was not just good. He was phenomenal. He dove to his left. He leaped higher than guys bigger than him could leap. He scrambled after grounders that other players would have let go on through for a hit. And his peg to first was a rocket. The first time he let loose, the first baseman almost dropped the ball it came in so hard.

The shortstop was a guy named Jimmy Masters. He joked with Scrapper as they jogged into the dugout.

"What a shame, kid. You got your nice new clean uniform all dirty."

"I hate clean uniforms!" Scrapper answered immediately.

Coach Cunningham heard this. He turned to his batting coach and winked.

The next inning out in the field, the Sox showed a little more hustle. The first guy up flied out deep. It was a good running catch by the right fielder.

"Come on!" Scrapper shouted as the second batter came up. "Let's get this guy!"

But the pitcher lost him on a three-two count and walked him. The next batter came up and smacked a bouncer over the bag at second. It looked like a sure single.

But Scrapper had been cheating toward the bag, and just when the ball should have gone bouncing out into center field, Scrapper was already diving for it. He grabbed the ball and fell to the ground. The runner from first was charging toward second.

The shortstop, Masters, had not reacted quickly. There was no time to feed the ball to him to get the force at second. Scrapper leaped to his feet and got to the bag just an instant before the runner came sliding in. Scrapper touched the bag with his foot, but as he jumped to avoid the slide, he felt something sharp and hard hit his leg.

But he didn't have time to think about it. Scrapper fired the ball off to first base. His throw beat the runner by a foot. Double play!

Coach Cunningham was smiling now as the team came in.

"Good hustle," he called out, clapping his hands together. "That's more like it."

Scrapper was the lead-off man. As he took his warm-up swings on deck, he realized that there was a cut on his left leg. It was sore and bleeding. The guy sliding into second had caught him with his cleats. Scrapper shrugged it off.

Minor-league injury. Major-league ball.

Scrapper felt good as he stepped into the batter's box. It already felt like a hundred years ago that he was sitting on the bench. He got a good grip on the bat and laced the very first pitch into left field for a hit.

As Scrapper hustled to first base, the pain in his leg hit him. He slowed up a little as he neared the bag, but then he saw that the left fielder was taking his time fielding the ball.

Mistake.

Scrapper suddenly took off, leg or no leg. He raced toward second. The left fielder saw what was happening. He snared the ball and whipped it into the infield. In the White Sox dugout, the guys were on their feet.

"Slide! Slide!"

Scrapper knew that he'd kill his leg if he slid in feet first. So he dove. He looked like Superman, sailing through the air. Scrapper hit the bag in a cloud of dirt, his head tucked down to avoid the tag.

"Safe!" the umpire called out.

The guys in the dugout cheered. Scrapper came home when the next batter went deep to right field. The third-base coach had to jump out of the way as Scrapper came flying around the bag.

The Sox lost the game eight to one. Back in the locker room, Coach Cunningham called the team together.

"Okay, guys. We've got twenty-nine more games to go down here in the Grapefruit League. After that, some of you guys are history. So it's put up or shut up. And I don't want to see the lame plays I saw the first half of this game."

Nobody said anything. Most of them looked down at the floor.

He looked around at the players. He stopped at Scrapper.

"You see this kid?" Cunningham said. Scrapper felt his face turning red. "Do you know who his father is?"

Scrapper tried to stop him. "Coach, wait a minute. I—"

"His father is Joe Mitchell."

This got the place buzzing. Faces turned to get another look at Scrapper.

"I don't have to tell you all how great Joe Mitchell was," Coach Cunningham went on. "Now, I'm not saying this kid's any Joe Mitchell. But he showed some good hustle out there today. The rest of you should check it out." He clapped his hands. "Okay, that's it. Get your showers."

Scrapper showered and dressed, then the team doctor bandaged up his leg. As Glen was leaving, Ted Leonard caught up with him. There was a guy behind him with a minicam.

"Say, Scrap. You got a minute?" Leonard asked.

Scrapper laughed. "Sure. I've got lots of them."

The guy with the minicam fiddled with a few of the knobs.

"That was pretty clever," Leonard said. "I mean, warming up with those oranges. The crowd liked it."

Scrapper shrugged, "You gotta do what you gotta do."

He couldn't believe he had just said that. That was his father's motto. It just came out.

The cameraman flipped on his light. Ted Leonard held up the microphone and looked into the camera.

"We're here in the White Sox locker room after the first game of spring training. I'm sorry to say that the Sox came up on the short end of this one. But the good news is that one of the team's hot new prospects showed some real hustle out there today. I'm talking about one of the three Rosemont boys who got drafted together last year. Glen 'Scrapper' Mitchell. Hey, Glen, great game today."

Scrapper shrugged. "Yeah," he said. "Just wait 'til tomorrow!"

FOUR

DT Green was off to a great start. He knew that he was in a groove. Lacing doubles, triples, and home runs in the first week of spring training, he was already the team RBI leader. When the Red Sox went on the road, Green roomed with Pete Kenney, the left fielder. When they'd get to the motel, Kenney liked to rib him.

"Hey, what are you unpacking your suitcase for, Shorty? You're practically on your way to Boston."

And Green felt it. *If I keep playing like this*, he thought, *they'll* have *to send me up*. He knew he shouldn't, but it was hard to keep himself from imagining his rookie year with the Boston Red Sox. Green knew exactly why Boston had wanted him. Fenway Park. The Green Monster. With that long, powerful swing of Green's—people were already saying it was like Dave Winfield's—he would be slamming the ball into the Green Monster all season long!

Green imagined the cheering fans. He imagined the reporters crowding around him in the locker room. He saw his face on TV. And the money! With the kind of spring he was capable of, he'd be able to negotiate a pretty fat contract. Wouldn't *that* be great! He could call his mom and tell her to quit one of her two jobs. Or, hey, quit them both! And then the endorsements. And the Rookie of the Year Award. And . . .

"Earth to Green. Earth to Green."

It was Pete Kenney. The team bus had just pulled into Lakeland, where they were going to play a weekend series against the Tigers. Green was staring out the window of the bus. But he wasn't seeing palm trees. He was seeing headlines.

"Look at Shorty!" Kenney called out to the other players. "The Invasion of the Body Snatchers got his brain!" Kenney rapped on Green's head with his knuckles. "Hello? Anybody home?"

The other players laughed, and Green joined them.

"Yeah, yeah," he said. "Very funny."

Somebody from the back of the bus called out, "He's dreaming about all the grand slams he's going to get in the World Series!" This time, Green felt himself turning a little red. The guy wasn't too far off.

Coach Brooks stood up in the front of the bus. As usual, he had that sour look on his face.

"Okay, ladies. You want me to pass out the

knitting or does anybody here maybe feel like playing a little ball!"

The players jumped to their feet and grabbed their bags. While Green was pulling his bag down off the rack, he mumbled to Pete Kenney, "Is that guy allergic to being friendly?"

Kenney shrugged. "Coach Brooks is what you call a sore winner. Don't let him get to you. He's all right."

"Well, if you say so."

The Tigers had a pretty nice stadium in Lakeland. It was bigger than the one the Red Sox played in at Winter Haven. It felt more to Green like what a real major-league stadium was like.

While Green was taking his batting practice, Pete Kenney came up to the cage. He had a weird look on his face.

"What's wrong?" Green joked. "Did you just look in the mirror?"

But Kenney didn't seem to hear him. "This place is jinxed," he said.

Green swung at the next pitch coming in and missed. The ball slammed against the back of the cage.

"What do you mean?" Green said.

"Jinxed," Kenney answered. "Spooked. Bad luck. They've been playing over a week here and so far no one has hit the ball over the fence."

Green looked over toward the outfield. There were advertisements running along the fence. Dead center was one for Marine World. It had a dolphin leaping out of the water. It looked almost like the dolphin was leaping up to try for a fly ball.

Another ball came in, and Green gave a lazy swing, knocking the ball to shallow right. Coach Brooks was walking past the batter's cage just then, and he stopped to listen in.

"You see that dolphin?" Green said to Kenney, pointing with his bat out toward the outfield wall. "I'll bet you an eighteen-inch pizza that I knock the ball right over that dolphin's head."

"Right now?" Kenney asked.

Green shook his head. "During the game. I'll break that jinx."

"A homer?"

"Yep." Another ball came in, and Green drove it to the alley in deep left. "Piece of cake," Green added.

While Green was laughing at this, another ball came in and whizzed right by him. It slammed against the cage. Green turned his head and saw Coach Brooks standing there.

"You're pretty sure of yourself, aren't you, Green?" Brooks said.

Pete Kenney heard something in the coach's voice he didn't like, and he spoke up quickly.

"Hey, Coach, Shorty's been doing okay so far. You gotta admit it."

Brooks pointed his finger at Kenney. "Yeah, and he might do just as well in *left* field, Kenney. You never know. Now I asked *him*, I didn't ask you." He turned back to Green. "So what about it?"

Green wasn't exactly sure what the coach was asking. But he had sure been noticing how Brooks wasn't much like Coach La Russo back in Chicago. La Russo used to jump around and scream and cheer like the rest of the guys whenever Green slapped a homer. He was in there a hundred and ten percent. But this guy was different. He just kind of grunted whenever Green did his thing.

"I'm hitting the ball pretty good, Coach," Green said finally.

"And you're talking about it pretty good, too," Brooks said.

Green said nothing. He recognized attitude when he saw it. And the coach was definitely coming at him with attitude. Green knew that Coach Brooks had never really been much as a player. Maybe that was it, Green thought. *I'm good and I know it. And he wasn't so good, and he knows it.*

Kenney spoke up for him again. "Hey, Coach. He's just doing his job."

Brooks hitched his thumbs in his belt loops and spat some tobacco onto the dirt. He jerked his head for Kenney to come closer.

In a low voice, Brooks told him, "And I'm just doing mine, Pete. You know that. You've been around."

Kenney nodded. Brooks spat again. He looked over at Green.

"Now, remember to keep your eyes on the third-base coach, Green. He calls the shots. I've seen you kind of going off on your own lately. We don't need that. There's nine people on this team, not just one."

The coach walked away.

"What's eating him?" Green asked.

Kenney didn't respond. "Hey, that reminds me. Is that pizza going to be with the works?"

Green laughed. "You tell me. You'll be buying."

"Yeah, we'll see."

The game ran scoreless into the eighth. A pitcher's duel. Even Green wasn't getting any good wood on the ball. He made a couple of good catches out in the field. He was feeling loose. It was just that no one was finding a groove against these two pitchers.

Green led off the top of the eighth. He could tell that the pitcher was getting tired. His first three pitches were all high. So was the fourth, but Green swung at it, anyway, getting a piece of it and fouling it off. The ball had cracked the bat, so Green hustled back to the dugout to get another one. Brooks met him there. He was angry.

"Green, keep your eye on the third-base coach, will you?" Brooks snapped. "Now he just told you to pass on that last pitch."

"Well . . . I—"

"You swung at a bad pitch is what you did. That would have been a walk, son. Now come on! Get in the game!"

Green walked back to the plate. His ears were burning. *Get in the game . . . son?* He spit on his hands and got a good grip on the bat. *What does he mean?* Green thought. *I'm hitting over .350. I'll show him who is in the game. I'm tired of this stuff.*

The pitch came in right down the middle. Green

whipped his bat. He creamed it. The ball flew out over the field and landed behind the fence . . . just over the nose of the leaping dolphin.

The guys in the dugout leaped to their feet.

"All right!"

Green rounded the bases at full speed, his fists pumping the air. Right over the dolphin's nose! So much for the jinx.

In the dugout, the guys were all over him, slapping his back and high-fiving him. Green high-fived Pete Kenney, then laughed.

"The works!"

Coach Brooks was down at the far end of the dugout. He tugged on his cap and spit some tobacco out onto the grass. He clapped his hands and yelled out to the next batter.

"Okay, keep it going."

He didn't say anything to Green. Ten minutes later, the game was over. Red Sox 1; Tigers 0

The Red Sox played the Tigers two more games, winning them both. A sweep. DT Green went five for nine for the series, adding another homer and a pair of doubles. After each hit, he came back into the dugout saying, "Piece of cake." By the time the team got on the bus and headed back to Winter Haven, where they had a pair of games to play against Oakland, Green had gotten a new nickname: Cake Man.

"Okay," Coach Brooks said to the team as the bus headed down the highway toward Winter Haven. "These guys beat us in the play-offs last year. As far as I'm concerned, this is a grudge match. I want heads-up ball out of everyone. No hot-dogging. This is the team to beat."

The team cheered. The sweep of the Tigers had really pumped them up. Green was psyched. He was going to make it! He could just feel it.

Coach Brooks stood quietly in the Red Sox dugout with his arms crossed on his chest. He was watching "Cake Man" Green as he trotted around the bases after *another* home run. Two in one game. The kid was hot.

It had been a long time since Ed Brooks could remember a rookie like this, someone who was ripping the cover off the ball almost every time he stepped up to the plate. Brooks thought back to his early days, when he was trying out for the Dodgers. There had been a guy back then—Rick the Stick, they called him—who reminded Brooks a little bit of this kid, Green. The Stick was pretty much a hotshot. He was good and he knew it. Brooks frowned as he remembered. The Stick had made the team his very first year out. Ed Brooks hadn't.

As Green trotted around third, he flashed a big thumbs-up to the bench. Up until now, the game had been tight, the lead going back and forth between the teams. But with two men on when Green clobbered the ball, it suddenly looked like the game was on ice.

The two guys who Green had knocked in were waiting at the plate. They all high-fived each other, then trotted toward the dugout. The crowd was still on its feet, some cheering, some booing. Green tipped his hat to them.

Coach Brooks suddenly snarled from the dugout. "Green! What do you think this is, a beauty pageant?

Green stopped short. "I was just—"

"Get in here!" the coach snapped. "I know what you were just doing."

The other players glanced nervously at Green as he came down into the dugout. The coach had been riding Cake Man for over a week now. So far, the young slugger had stayed cool. But a guy has only got so much patience.

Green took a few steps toward the coach. Because he was taller by a good six inches, Green had to look down at the coach when he talked to him.

"What did I do wrong, Coach?" he asked. "We're ahead, aren't we? Isn't that the idea?"

Brooks glared at him a long time before he answered.

"I want ballplayers on my teams. Not stars."

Green's mouth dropped open.

"What?"

But the case was closed. The coach went to the far side of the dugout. Green looked around at the other players. A few of them shrugged. A few others looked away. Only Pete Kenney seemed loose about the whole thing. He made an ultra-serious face at Green—impersonating Brooks— then tipped his cap. But Green didn't dare laugh.

Oakland got those three runs back with a rally

in the seventh, then added two more on an error. Brooks was fuming.

"You get a lead, you protect it!" he yelled at his players.

Green had done his part in the Oakland half of the eighth, playing the bounce off the wall just right on a hard outfield hit, then gunning the runner down at second with a perfect throw.

"Okay, now," Brooks called out as his team came in to bat. "Now or never. Let's go!"

Pete Kenney led off, smashing the ball toward the third baseman. The ball took a funny bounce, and Kenney legged it out, beating the throw. Infield hit.

The next guy flied out. Green watched from the on-deck circle. He was swinging a pair of bats. A home run would tie it up. And that was exactly what Green planned on hitting. He laughed to himself. Piece of cake.

But as Green started for the plate, the third-base coach trotted down to him.

"Keep your eye on me, now," he said. "They know you're a long-baller. They'll be playing you to swing away."

Green nodded. "They'll need wings. I'm going to crush it."

The coach frowned. "Wrong. You're going to bunt."

Green couldn't believe it. "What?"

"You heard me. Bunt. Now remember the signal. I touch my elbow and my ear."

"But—"

"Get up there."

The umpire had started over. The third-base coach waved him off.

"It's okay, Lou, we're just trying to figure out how far he should hit it."

The umpire laughed. The third-base coach hustled back to his position and called out to Green, "Okay. Let them have it!"

He was bluffing. But it was working. The Oakland infielders were edging back onto the grass. The outfielders were drifting toward the fence.

Green stepped in and took a few powerful swings. He felt great. Loose. He wanted to go for the homer. He glanced down at the third-base coach. The guy looked like he had ants running up and down the inside of his uniform. He was slapping his hands all over the place. But Green saw the signal. Elbow. Ear. The bunt was definitely on.

The pitcher set and delivered. Green's mind said, "Bunt!" but his body wasn't listening. Before he knew what he was doing, Green took a mighty cut at the ball, and missed. He couldn't believe he had done it.

"Strike one!"

Green glanced down at the third-base coach. The coach glared back at him. He was slapping himself all over. Again, he went for the elbow and the ear.

Okay, Green thought. *Here goes.*

The pitch came in. This time, Green squared to bunt. He pushed the bat out and topped the ball, then took off for first base as fast as he could. Out of the corner of his eye, though, he saw the pitcher kneel down casually and field the ball. It was a lousy bunt!

The pitcher turned and fired to second before Kenney had even started on his slide. The shortstop took the throw, scraped his foot across the bag, and fired off to first. His throw beat Green by a good four steps.

Double play. The game was over.

Back in the locker room, nobody was patting Cake Man Green on the back. No one was saying anything now about his two homers, his three RBIs, his great rocket to second from the outfield. A few of the guys were slamming their lockers shut. A reporter came, but he was chased away. Who wants to talk about losing?

And Green knew he was in hot water for sure for swinging at that first pitch when he had been told to bunt.

An hour later he was standing in Coach Brooks's office. The coach was sitting behind his desk, going after his fingernails with a large pair of scissors. He looked up, as if he hadn't even seen Green walk in. There was something wrong with the way he was smiling. He looked too calm. And then he frowned.

"Close the door, kid." he said.

FIVE

Scrapper Mitchell dove to his right and smothered the ball. Dust flew everywhere. He scrambled to his knees and fired the ball to first.

Out!

Scrapper and the third baseman had a runner caught in a rundown. Scrapper pumped his arm, faking a throw, and the runner broke for the bag. Scrapper practically tackled him.

Out!

Next, it was a short pop to shallow center. The center fielder was trotting in to take the ball on the hop. Suddenly, Scrapper came barreling out onto the grass. He caught the ball on a dead run, then smashed into the center fielder. They both went down. The center fielder lost one of his front teeth. But Scrapper held on to the ball.

That was the end of the video tape. There were

about five seconds of some of the guys clowning around, then the screen turned to static. Coach Cunningham turned off the TV set while one of the other players flipped on the lights in the meeting room.

"Hey!" someone yelled. "Who is that guy? I want his autograph!"

The guy who had yelled was Scrapper himself. He noticed right away that only about half the other players were laughing at his joke. Chris Wilson, the center fielder, was one of the guys not laughing. A guy with a missing front tooth looks pretty strange when he laughs.

Coach Cunningham looked out at his players.

"That guy," he said sternly, "was a hot dog."

Scrapper looked up sharply.

"Hey, I caught the ball!"

Cunningham looked at him. "I know you caught the ball, Mitchell. Do you think I don't have eyes?"

Scrapper shrugged. "Sure, you've got eyes, Coach."

Coach Cunningham smirked. "Well, thank you."

A couple of the guys laughed. The coach went on.

"Now, since you've got such great eyes, suppose you tell us what you did wrong on that last play?"

Scrapper answered immediately. "Did wrong? That's simple. Nothing."

Coach Cunningham looked over at Chris Wilson.

"How about you, Wilson? What went wrong with that play?"

Wilson glared over at Scrapper. "I got my tooth knocked out by that creep, that's what."

"Aw, you got plenty more where that came from," Scrapper shot back.

Wilson leaped to his feet. So did Scrapper.

"You feel like losing one of yours?" Wilson yelled.

"Just try!"

Chairs skidded against the floor as the guys in between them quickly moved out of the way. But before the two players could go at it, Coach Cunningham yelled for them to stop.

"One move from either of you and you're suspended! Now sit down!"

They did. Cunningham turned the TV back on and hit the reverse button on the VCR. A second later, the picture showed Scrapper falling back to the ground, where Wilson was, and then the two of them leaping *off* the ground and moving backward. It looked pretty funny, like a old-timey movie, and a couple of the players laughed. Scrapper wasn't one of them.

"Right here," Cunningham said. He hit a button on the VCR and froze the picture. "Now, one of you two tell me. At this point, who called for the ball?"

No one answered.

"Wilson, did you call for the ball?"

Wilson glared up at the coach. "No," he grumbled.

"How about you, Mitchell? Did you wave him off?"

Scrapper exploded. "What do you mean, 'wave

him off"! I was running a hundred miles an hour! He can wave himself off! I made the play!"

"But you shouldn't have had to," Cunningham said. He looked at everybody. "There's a thing called teamwork. It doesn't mean you don't hustle. But it does mean you don't get in the other guy's way when he's got a play. You should know that by now."

Scrapper couldn't believe it. *What is it with the majors?* he wondered. *You catch a ball, they climb all over you.*

Coach Cunningham flipped off the TV.

"Wilson, you should have called for the ball. That was your play. It was in front of you. But you, Mitchell. Even if the he *had* called for it, the tape shows that you would have probably still plowed right into him, anyway. Hustling is fine. Lost teeth are not. You guys are no good to me if you're on the disabled list. Now that's it."

The meeting was over. As the players filed out of the conference room, Scrapper found himself next to Wilson.

"You're a hot dog," Wilson grumbled.

Scrapper laughed him off. "You're nuts."

"You watch who you're calling nuts!"

Scrapper stopped and opened his eyes real wide.

"Yep," he said. "You're still nuts."

Wilson didn't think that was so funny, but before he could do anything, a couple of the veteran players had moved in between the two.

"Come on, kiddies," Jimmy Masters said. "If you gotta fight, go out in the sandbox."

Scrapper put his face up to Wilson's.

"Remember, man. I *caught* it."

Ever since he was a kid and turned his first single into a sliding triple, Scrapper played to win. His father had always told him, "Play every game like it's your last." Only, Scrapper had modified that. He played every *play* like it was his last. He figured that was the only way he would ever see his plaque up there on the wall in the Baseball Hall of Fame, next to his dad's someday.

Some of the players had been ribbing him about his father. Whenever Scrapper struck out or flied out, there was one guy who almost always called out, "Hey, you ought to borrow your dad's bat! It worked pretty good!"

Scrapper could never understand why they always talked about his bat, never about his glove. He didn't like to say it out loud to anyone, but as far as fielding went, Scrapper had his dad beat.

Practice went pretty well. Scrapper and the short-stop, Jimmy Masters, got into a competition during grounder drills to see who could get to the ball faster. They were pretty even.

Coach Cunningham called his players together after the practice. He had an announcement to make.

"All right, we've got a little tradition down here in spring training. We call it 'separating the men from the boys.'"

A couple of the guys nudged each other and joked.

"That leaves you out."

"Very funny."

The coach went on. "It's really a lot simpler than it sounds. It's rookies versus veterans. Full scrimmage."

The rookies looked around at each other, sizing up their chances. Scrapper could tell by the grins on the veterans' faces that they were figuring to lap these guys up.

"And there's something I should tell you new guys," Coach Cunningham added. "We've been doing this for ten years now. And the vets have never lost yet."

Scrapper piped up, "Well, there's always a first time!"

The veterans laughed at this.

"Hey, look. Joe junior thinks he's going to take us to the cleaners."

The other guys picked up on it.

"Say, Junior, you think you can get me your dad's autograph?"

"Yeah. How about it, Junior?"

Scrapper didn't answer any of them. His face turned bright red, but he kept his mouth shut. *Save it for the game*, he told himself. *Save it for the game*.

Scrapper's parents called that night to see how things were coming along. Scrapper didn't mention anything about his getting taunted. He told his father about the scrimmage.

"Oh, yeah," Joe Mitchell said. "The old green

and gray. We used to do that when I was with the Phillies."

"Green and gray?"

"Sure. Rookies used to be called greenhorns. They'd call them the greens."

"But what's the gray?"

Joe Mitchell laughed his big, booming laugh. "Gray old men, son! What else?" Joe Mitchell paused to get a laugh from his son. When he didn't, he continued. "Now, kidding aside, this green and gray game isn't just so that the coaches can get a good look at you new guys. They watch the veterans sharply to see if they've lost anything over the winter. Those guys'll be playing hard. It's their position on the team."

"But, Dad, Coach said it's just a tradition to keep the team edge. Maybe when you were playing . . ."

"It hasn't changed, son, take it from me," Joe Mitchell said angrily. "And you better step closer into the box when you're hitting and keep—"

"My eye on the pitcher. Yeah, Dad. You told me a million times."

"And about your base coverage, you should . . ."

Glen Mitchell resigned himself to another lecture.

Out in the dugout the next day, Coach Cunningham watched as the rookies took the field. They were chattering away, jiving each other, tossing the ball back and forth, pounding their mitts . . . Cunningham's veteran catcher came up to him.

"What's got into them?"

Cunningham shrugged. But he had a pretty good idea, anyway.

The game was a free-for-all. Hitters on both squads were hot. Out in the field, guys were making incredible running catches. Scrapper and Chris Wilson got on base in the third and executed a perfect double steal. Then Scrapper danced around on second base enough to draw a throw from the pitcher, and Wilson stole home.

The game strayed close into the middle innings. Everyone's adrenaline was pumping. Because it was just an intrasquad game, there wasn't much of a crowd. But whoever was there was seeing some of the wildest baseball ever. And they loved it. When Scrapper turned a tricky bouncer into a double play to kill a potentially big inning for the veterans, the small crowd cheered as if it were the World Series.

At his next at bat, Scrapper couldn't resist pulling what he called his "flip flap." His father would be mad, but who cared? After the first pitch—which Scrapper let pass as a called strike—he stepped over the plate to the opposite side, and settled in left handed.

"Hey! He can't do that!" the catcher yelled.

"I'm switch-hitting," Scrapper said. "I sure can."

"It's weird," the umpire said. "But I guess he can do it."

The catcher stood up and started to protest some more, but the crowd began to boo.

"Forget it," the umpire said. "Play ball."

Scrapper took a ball high. Then he stepped back over the plate again. The crowd went nuts.

"Hey, are you going to do that all day?" the umpire asked.

Scrapper pumped his bat. He didn't answer.

And he didn't have to. The next pitch had "Hit me" written all over it. Scrapper swung. Crack! The ball fell into the gap in left center and went rolling to the wall. Scrapper had a stand-up double. But he slid, anyway.

Jimmy Masters trotted over to the bag to take the throw from the outfield.

"You again," he said.

Scrapper dusted himself off. "Me again."

In the end, the veterans got their big bats going. A pair of homers in the ninth iced the game. The rookies lost 10–7. The small crowd gave the rookies a standing ovation, anyway.

Back in the locker room, everyone was dead tired, but in a great mood. Scrapper had just started to pull off his shirt when Chris Wilson and two other guys grabbed hold of him and dragged him into the showers. Scrapper didn't even fight back. He got soaking wet, clothes and all. It felt great. Scrapper couldn't remember ever feeling this good after *losing* a game.

When Scrapper got out of the shower, he noticed a bunch of guys gathered over near his locker. Chris Wilson backed away from the pack and came over to him.

"Hey, Mitch. A guy from *Sports Illustrated* is here! And he wants to talk to you!"

Scrapper tightened his towel, and went over to his locker. A blond guy was there holding a notebook.

"You're Glen Mitchell?"

Scrapper nodded. "Yeah."

"Joe Mitchell's son?"

Scrapper frowned. "What's this about?"

The reporter opened his notebook. "Well, look. We're doing a special father/son issue of *SI*, and we'd like to talk to you about your—"

Scrapper cut him off. "Sorry, I'm not interested." He pushed past the reporter and opened his locker.

But the guy persisted. "But your dad said we could contact you."

Scrapper took out his toilet kit and slammed his locker door. "Look, I really don't have the time for interviews right now. I'm in training. My father should have thought about that. Thanks, anyway."

He walked into the washroom, leaving the reporter with his mouth open.

SIX

"Strike three! Yer out!"

The batter turned and headed back toward the dugout. Halfway there he threw his bat to the ground, and then his batting helmet. He pulled off his batting glove and threw *it* to the ground, too. The next batter up was coming out of the on-deck circle.

"What's he throwing?" he asked.

"That's what I'd like to know."

What Magic Ramirez was throwing was a fastball, a sinker, a slider and a change-up that had most of the batters in the Grapefruit League swinging at air. The Dodgers were ecstatic. The kid from Rosemont was the hottest thing since Valenzuela. In his last four outings, Magic had posted three shutouts, one of them a no-hitter into the seventh.

As the next batter dug in, Magic leaned in for the sign. The catcher was grinning. He wanted the screwball. Magic took a deep breath. It was very strange what was happening to him down here in Florida. He had the most wins and the lowest ERA of any pitcher on the Dodger staff. He was averaging seven strikeouts a game. And no one yet had hit a home run off him.

But still, he was kind of worried. It all seemed too good. Too perfect. When you're on top, there's only one place to go.

Magic flipped the ball around in his hand, squeezing his knuckles against the seams. Screwball. It was probably as hard to throw as it was to hit. Magic was having a little trouble lately keeping his screwball from tailing up and in.

Ramirez rocked and fired. The moment the ball left his hand, it felt all wrong. Sure enough, as he looked up from his follow-through he saw that the ball was drifting high. The batter stayed with it until the last instant, then hit the dirt to avoid being beaned. The ball slammed against the back fence.

The Dodgers' catcher, Ben Porter, trotted out to the mound with a new ball.

"Hey, what was that?"

Magic tried to shrug it off. "I'm okay."

"I didn't ask that. What happened? Did you lose your grip?"

Magic shook his head. "Let's just forget the screwball today, okay? It's not working."

The catcher looked at him a second.

"Okay. You're the boss."

He dropped the ball in Magic's glove and went back to take up his position behind the plate.

Magic pitched flawlessly the rest of the game. The Dodgers won 3–1. Not such a great score. But still, a win was a win. Magic Ramirez was now five and oh. Not too shabby.

Back at the motel, Magic sat on his bed soaking his elbow in ice. The TV was on, but Magic wasn't really paying attention to it. He was thinking about the screwball and about how close it came to hitting the batter. *What if I lose my control?* Magic was thinking. *What if all this is a fluke?* Getting into the major leagues meant everything to Magic right now. And so far, with this incredible spring he was having, it actually seemed possible.

Outside, some of his teammates were in the motel's swimming pool, and doing cannonballs off the diving board and yelling and laughing. As Magic adjusted the ice on his elbow, he suddenly heard a chant start up from outside.

"Ma-gic! Ma-gic! Ma-gic!"

Magic hopped off the bed and hurried over to the window. A big smile grew on his face.

Ben Porter was standing in the shallow end of the pool, wearing his Dodgers cap. Up on the diving board, about six of the guys were lined up. Porter was pretending to pitch, copying Magic's motion. And each time he followed through, the next guy in line would take a huge cut with an imaginary bat and fall into the water. It was hilarious. Porter had Magic's style down perfectly. Each time another guy hit the water, the rest of them chanted, "Mag-ic! Mag-ic!"

Finally, Porter yelled out something that Magic couldn't hear, and then he went into the most exaggerated windup yet. He made the "pitch." There were four guys up on the diving board. They all swung at once, and went splashing down into the water. It looked like when the bad guys are shot off the roof in the old Westerns.

Magic chuckled to himself. Four strikeouts with one pitch. He imagined the headline: Ramirez Does the Impossible.

Immediately he stopped smiling. *Don't jinx it,* he said to himself.

Magic went over to the TV and flipped the channel to MTV. *There,* he thought. *Now I can forget about baseball for a little bit.* He sat back down on the bed. The next video up was one of the old ones. Bruce Springsteen's "Glory Days," the one where the Boss is playing baseball.

"All right!"

Magic sat up on the bed and grabbed a ball off the table next to him. He didn't make a move to change the channel.

Ramirez was all geared up that Monday. The White Sox were due in for a pair of games. It would be the first time that Magic had seen Scrapper since they had all come down to Florida.

Magic was due to pitch the second game, so he sat on the bench in the dugout for the first and watched as Scrapper outhustled almost everybody else on the field. A couple of times, Magic forgot where he was, and he almost cheered when

Scrapper came up with a great play. The other guys on the bench were muttering about "that hot dog." Magic couldn't wait to tell him.

After the game, Magic met Scrapper out in the parking lot.

"Hey, show-off!"

"Hey, dead-arm!"

They high-fived each other, then dropped to a crouch, like boxers, and rabbit-punched each other a few times.

"So how's life as a Dodger, you traitor?" Scrapper joked.

"Hey, you guys could still get me—" Magic answered, "for a cool million."

"In your dreams, Ramirez."

"Yeah. That is, if I don't get cut."

"Are you crazy? They're not going to cut *you*. Don't you read the papers? Mr. Shutout. You're in there, Magic. No sweat. You'll make it."

"I don't know . . ."

"Well, I do. You've got a bionic arm. What team wouldn't want that?"

"I hope so."

Scrapper shook his head. "Same old Magic. You still like anchovies on your pizza, or have you finally turned normal?"

"Very funny."

"Well?"

"I still like them."

Scrapper held his nose and made a face. "Well, if you keep 'em off my side, I say we split a pie."

Magic rolled his eyes and smiled. "Sounds great."

After the pizza, Scrapper asked Magic, "What do you do for fun around here?"

Magic scratched his head. "How about the beach?"

Scrapper slapped him five. "I can handle it."

They took a bus to the beach, which was only a couple miles away. There was a boardwalk there, and they played a few video games in one of the arcades.

"It's pretty weird, isn't it?" Magic said to Scrapper after they had left the video arcade and were walking down the boardwalk.

"What? That I'm better at Turbo and Invaders than you are?"

"Funny. No, I mean about being down here. I still can't believe I'm really playing with the Dodgers. It's like I'm going to wake up any minute and I'll be in Mr. Weber's dumb English class and realize I've just fallen asleep in class, and all this is a dream."

Scrapper laughed at that. "You *did* used to fall asleep in Mr. Weber's class!"

"Can you blame me?"

"No," said Scrapper. "But I know what you mean. I always thought that because of my dad and everything, that I sort of knew what being in the big leagues would feel like. But it's a lot different than I thought."

"Yeah, tell me about it."

"I'm already sick of motels."

"And buses."

"Yeah. I figured by now we'd be riding in limos."

Magic laughed. "You don't ask for much, do you, Scrap?"

They walked on a little farther. Up ahead were some rides and game booths in a small amusement park called Playland. A big Ferris wheel with green and yellow lights was slicing through the air. As they passed by the game booths, the guys behind the counters were yelling out over their cheap microphones.

"Come on, give it a try. Only a dollar. Try your luck. Win a prize. Only a dollar."

Scrapper and Magic stepped up to one of the games. It was called Jungle Hunt. The back of the game booth was a fake jungle with a bunch of plastic animals in it. A lion, a tiger, some monkeys, and a giraffe—each with a hole in its mouth, the size of a baseball.

"Try your luck. Only a buck."

"What's the deal on this one?" Scrapper asked.

The guy behind the counter answered, "Get the ball in the mouth, win a prize. The more you get, the bigger the prize."

"What's the biggest prize you've got?" Scrapper asked.

The guy reached up and pulled down a gigantic stuffed gorilla. The thing was *ugly*.

"You get them all, you win the gorilla," he said.

Scrapper was already reaching into his pocket for a dollar.

"What do you say, Ramirez," he said to Magic, winking. "Do you think you know how to throw a baseball?"

Magic stepped up to the counter and picked up one of the balls.

"Well . . . I guess I could try."

"Go on," the guy said. "You never know. You might get lucky."

Magic hesitated. "Well, I don't know."

"Go ahead. What have you got to lose?"

He reared back and fired the ball.

Five minutes later, Magic was walking down the boardwalk carrying the huge gorilla. The guy behind the counter sat and stared. Scrapper and Magic were cracking up.

"That guy's mouth dropped open so wide you could have tossed a baseball in *it*!" Scrapper said.

Magic was struggling under the huge gorilla.

"What am I going to do with this thing?" he asked.

Scrapper thought a second, then snapped his fingers.

"We'll send it to Green!"

Magic laughed. "Mr. Mitchell, you are brilliant."

Magic pitched the next day. He was in good form, retiring the first six batters he faced.

Scrapper led off the top of the third. Magic could tell from the intense look on his friend's face as he settled in at the plate that Scrapper had no intention of being an easy out. Scrapper crowded the plate. There were no smiles now.

The count ran to three and two, and then Scrapper fouled off the next pitch. Then he fouled off the next one. And then the next one. And the one after that.

Ben Porter called time and came out to the mound.

"This guy's got your number. Give him your heat. Split-finger fast. Inside corner."

But Scrapper fouled that one off, too. Magic bore down. He threw again. And then again. He even tried the knuckler. It was perfect, skittering around like a hot potato. But it didn't work. Scrapper stayed with it, got a piece of it, and fouled it off. The players in the White Sox dugout were on their feet, cheering their second baseman on. After the tenth straight foul, the Dodgers got up and started to cheer Magic on.

"Blow it past him, Ramirez!"

"Burn it!"

Finally, Porter trotted back out to the mound. He looked into the Dodger dugout to get a sign.

"Forget this guy," he said to Magic. "He's an animal. He'll wear your arm off if he keeps this up. Just pitch around him."

"You mean walk him?"

"Yeah. We'll be here all day. Just toss it wide. We'll try to get the next guy to hit into a double play. But this is crazy. You must've thrown this guy ten pitches."

He went back and took up his position behind the plate. Magic wound, and threw wide. The ball trailed away the instant it left his hand. Ben Porter scooted over to take the throw.

But Scrapper wasn't finished yet. Gripping the bat at the very bottom, Scrapper lunged over the plate and took a wild swing at the ball—and got it. The ball blooped over the first baseman's head and ran down the line.

Magic stood on the mound and watched as his buddy legged his way to first. Magic realized that he should have known better. If there was one thing that Scrapper hated more than anything, it was the intentional walk. Scrapper would rather strike out swinging than be given a free pass.

The right fielder was slow getting to the ball. Mistake. When Scrapper saw this, he turned on the juice and went chugging around first. The right fielder got to the ball, but bobbled it. There was no chance for a play at second. But Scrapper didn't know that.

Suddenly, Magic yelled out, "*Slide!*"

Scrapper did, diving face first into the bag in a cloud of dirt. A full five seconds later, the ball came in from the outfield. Scrapper got up and dusted himself off. He glared over at Magic, who just shrugged and turned away to face the next batter.

Next batter, Magic caught his friend off guard and picked him off with a lightning-fast move. Scrapper kicked himself the whole way back to the dugout.

SEVEN

"Hey, Cake Man! Over here!" "Me! Cake! Sign here!" "Hey! Cake!"

Green stood at the fence behind home plate, signing autographs. It still felt kind of strange, but he liked it.

"Cake, how about a picture?"

Green laughed. "Sure."

The kid who had asked slipped under the rail and stood next to Green. He came up to the ballplayer's belt. His friend held up the camera and snapped it.

"All right!" the friend said. "How about me, now?"

Green shrugged. "Why not?"

Someone else had shoved another piece of paper and a pencil at him.

"Who's this one to?" Green asked.

"Put down 'To Tom.'"

Green put the pencil against his chin. "Hmmm. I'm not sure I can spell that one."

The kids cracked up.

Over in the dugout, Coach Brooks was watching. Pete Kenney came up to him.

"Looks like someone's got himself a fan club," he said.

Brooks nodded. "Looks like."

The kid who had taken the picture scrambled up next to Green for his turn to get his picture taken. Green took off his Red Sox cap and stuck it on the kid's head. The two of them laughed.

Kenney said nothing. It seemed like the better Cake Man Green hit the ball, the more Brooks climbed all over him. The guy just didn't let up.

And neither did Green. Green was tearing up the league with his bat. His batting average was getting closer and closer to .350. He was swatting the ball to all fields . . . and out of most of the parks. The only other rookie even close was a guy named Ken Taylor, with Toronto. But so far Green was on top. Though you'd never have known it, the way Brooks was riding him.

One of the Boston papers had done a story on Green, calling him "The *new* Big Green Monster." Green had cut the story out and sent it home to his mother. He was sure that she would put it up on the refrigerator door and show all the neighbors. Along with the story was a picture of Green in his classic home-run swing. The caption under the picture read: "More Icing from the Cake."

And as he always did when he wrote home,

Green had dropped a check into the envelope. Half his salary. It would help out a lot.

The game that day was against the Brewers. During batting practice, word ran among the Red Sox players that the first cut was going to be made after the game. A couple of the rookies looked pretty bummed. They knew they'd be getting the ax.

But when the Red Sox took the field, Green was surprised to find even Pete Kenney being quieter than usual. He tossed the ball around without his usual chatter. Sure, Kenney hadn't been having the greatest spring, but he'd get it together. Green figured there was no way the veteran left fielder would get cut.

Green didn't say anything to the left fielder about it, but having Kenney being so quiet kind of spooked Green. When the game started, Green misjudged the first fly ball that came his way. He started in when he should have gone back, and it dropped in for a single. Kenney backed him up on the play.

"Heads up!" he said sharply, as he threw the ball into second.

Coach La Russo, back in Rosemont, had said it plenty of times, and it was true: There's nothing like nerves to turn arms and legs into Jell-O. The Red Sox played one of their worst games all spring. By the fifth inning, the Brewers were coasting on a six-run lead. And to make it worse, the sky was getting dark. Huge purple-and-gray rainclouds were beginning to roll in.

In the sixth inning, Coach Brooks stood down at the far end of the dugout with his arms crossed, and watched Pete Kenney strike out for the last out of the inning. The rain was starting to fall now. Big fat drops. Green grabbed Kenney's glove to take it out to him. But Coach Brooks stopped him.

"Leave the glove. I'm giving Kenney a rest."

He turned to one of the other players—one of the rookies who was pretty certain to be cut—and told him to go out and play left field.

Green hadn't moved from the top step of the dugout. He was looking at Pete Kenney, who was taking his time coming back from the plate. Green had never seen Kenney looking so down.

"What's wrong? You get a little rain in your eyes?"

But Kenney didn't answer. Instead, Coach Brooks turned to Green.

"Green, are you waiting for a police escort, or can you find your own way to center field?"

Green took the hint. As he ran out onto the field, he thought he heard something behind him that sounded like someone throwing a bat into the dugout.

The rain was really coming down now. Walls of water blew across the field. The crowd was starting to head for cover.

The first batter up hit a blooper over the glove of the leaping shortstop. It looked like a sure single. But the new left fielder came charging in on the wet grass and dove for the ball. He caught it and went skidding along the grass about ten feet. It was a great catch, but hardly anyone had even seen it.

The left fielder got up off the grass and threw the ball back in. He turned to Green and shrugged his shoulders. Green knew exactly what the guy meant: too little, too late.

A minute later the game was called. Because they had completed the regulation five innings, it was an official game.

Brewers, six. Red Sox, nothing.

The locker room was unusually quiet. The players pretty much kept to themselves as they showered and dressed. No kidding around.

The players who were being cut were called into Coach Brooks's office one at a time. Green noticed that they weren't in there for long. He guessed that there really wasn't much to be said.

You're out. Sorry. Good luck.

It wasn't until he was showered and dressed that Green saw Pete Kenney. Kenney was over by the water fountain. Green went over to him. He didn't dare ask, and it was hard to tell from Kenney's face just what was what.

"Well," Kenney said. "The old coach has made a big mistake."

Green didn't respond.

Suddenly, the left fielder broke into his usual grin.

"Yeah," he said, laughing. "A b-i-g mistake. He's keeping me! Check it out!"

He held up both his hands, and Green slapped them as hard as he could.

"You're kidding! Hey, that's great!"

That night, Pete Kenney and Green and a couple of the other guys went out to the local triplex. The guy who took tickets recognized them. He was a Red Sox fan.

"Look," he told them. "When this movie's over, you can go over to the next theater and check that one out. It's all right. Nobody comes out on a rainy night like this. Go ahead."

And they did. They took in all three movies. With the rain still falling, they figured tomorrow's game would be canceled, anyway.

Pete Kenney insisted that each of them get a bucket of popcorn for each movie. He *dared* them to eat a whole bucket for each flick. No one turned down the dare.

It was after two o'clock in the morning when they finally left the theater, groaning from too much popcorn. They looked up at the sky. The rain had stopped, and there were a thousand stars in the sky.

"Uh-oh," said one of the guys. "You know what that means."

They sure did. It meant that tomorrow's game would be on, after all. The guys got back to the motel just before three o'clock. They were all still holding their stomachs.

"I feel like a hundred-and-ninety-five-pound piece of popcorn," Green said.

"You look like one," Kenney joked lamely.

"Don't. It hurts when I laugh."

"Who's laughing?"

* * *

Morning came too soon. Green was still out cold
when Kenney pounded on his door. Green called
out from under his pillow.

"Go away!"

"Get up!" Kenney yelled through the door.
"We're late!"

"Tell the coach I died."

"Suit yourself," Kenney said, and left.

As soon as Green arrived at the ball park, he
wished he *had* died. The rest of the team was
suited up and out on the field already, warming up.
Brooks caught Green sneaking into the locker
room.

"Well, so nice of you to join us, Mr. Green,"
Brooks said sarcastically. "And how are you this
morning? Or should I say, this afternoon?"

Green tried for a lame joke. "Do I look as bad as
I feel?"

Brooks checked him out. "The question is, are
you going to play as bad as you look?"

And he did. Trying to run down fly balls in the
outfield, Green felt as though his legs were lead.
His bat, too. Green couldn't come around on the
ball all afternoon. He went zero for four, striking
out twice and hitting a pair of weak pop-ups that
his own grandmother could have caught.

In the field, he committed his first official error
of spring training. A routine grounder bounced his
way, and he let the ball go right between his legs.

"Good thing cuts were yesterday and not today," Green said to Kenney as the two headed for the dugout after the final out.

"Don't look now," Kenney said. "But I think your biggest fan is waiting for you."

It was Coach Brooks. He was leaning against the dugout, and he waved Green over to him. He was smiling—sort of.

"Nice game, kid," he said sarcastically.

Green stammered, "Well, I just . . . I mean—"

The coach interrupted him. "I just thought you'd be interested to hear that Ken Taylor went four for four today over in Fort Lauderdale. Six RBIs, a homer, and a pair of doubles."

Green didn't say anything. He knew what the coach was up to.

"That puts him up around three-fifty," Brooks went on. "Do you know what your average is after today's incredible performance?"

Green mumbled, "No."

"Well, I'll tell you. It ain't no three-fifty. Not by a long shot."

Green looked his coach right in the eye.

"I had a bad game. What can I say?"

Brooks exploded. "I don't care what you say. I just care what you do! When it comes down to one final game in a pennant race, Green, let me tell you what I *don't* want on my team. I don't want a player who shows up two hours late, then just says 'hey, I had a bad game.' You can lose an entire season with a bad game. Now, look, we've got more cuts to make before spring training is over.

You're good, Green. But if you fade in the stretch . . ."

The coach didn't finish his sentence. Instead, he turned and headed off toward the clubhouse.

Green was stunned. He watched the dark form of the coach move off down the runway. Despite all the great things that had been happening to him this spring, the terrible thought came to him for the first time: *He might not make the team.*

EIGHT

Scrapper sat up on the metal table biting his lip while the team doctor smeared iodine on his latest cut. This one was on his left leg, just below the knee. It looked a lot like the one just above the knee. Scrapper had gotten that one the day before stealing second.

"We've got to stop meeting like this," the doctor joked as he got out a bandage to put over the cut.

But Scrapper was in a hurry. He didn't have time for any bandages.

"No stitches?" he asked.

"Stitches?" the doc said. "Not this time. But I think—"

"Thanks."

Scrapper rolled his pants leg down over the cut and hopped off the table.

"Slow down now," the doctor warned. "It

71

doesn't need stitches, but it's still a pretty deep cut."

But Scrapper had already grabbed his cap and glove and was limping back down the runway toward the dugout. The doctor just shook his head. The only thing that would stop this Mitchell kid was a full-blown broken leg. He put the lid back on the iodine bottle and corrected himself. No. *Two* broken legs.

Scrapper came into the dugout, trying his best not to limp. He was glad to see that his team was still up to bat.

"How many outs?" he called out.

One of the players answered, "Just one. Wilson's on first. Got a single."

Great, thought Scrapper. He hobbled to the home plate side of the dugout to watch the action. Coach Cunningham was there.

"How's the leg?" Cunningham asked.

"Fine," Scrapper answered. "No problem." He beat his fist against his leg. It did hurt, but he didn't show it. "I can still play."

Coach Cunningham wondered why he had even asked. There was a better chance that the sky would turn green than Scrapper Mitchell would voluntarily put himself on the bench.

"We had better give it a rest, though," Cunningham said. "Just to be careful."

Scrapper was all over him. "No way! I gotta keep it moving, or it'll freeze up!"

"Did the doctor tell you that?" Cunningham asked suspiciously.

Scrapper knew that he had better not lie.

"Well . . . I think he meant to. Look, Coach, it's a little cut. Big deal. I mean, come on. He didn't even put a bandage on it."

Cunningham rolled his eyes and looked up at the sky.

"Okay, Mitchell," he said. "If you want to stay in the game and kill yourself, be my guest."

That was all the Scrapper needed to hear. He turned his attention to the batter. Jimmy Masters was up. Scrapper called out to him.

"Come on, Masters! Knock it outta here!"

Two pitches later, Masters hit a frozen rope into the gap in left center. Wilson held up at second. This meant that Scrapper was on deck. He scrambled out of the dugout, clapping his hands for the next batter.

"Come on, come on! Keep it alive!"

But on the first pitch, the batter swung and popped up foul behind the plate. The catcher tore off his mask and went after it. The only problem was, the ball was coming down right in the on-deck circle, where Scrapper was taking his warm-up swings. And Scrapper didn't budge.

The catcher never saw him. He had his eye on the ball the whole time. He slammed into Scrapper at full speed, and the two players went down. The ball dropped to the ground.

"You jerk!" the catcher snarled.

"Hey, *jerk*," Scrapper snapped back, "can't you look where you're going?"

No more was said. The catcher threw a punch that caught Scrapper just under the eye. Scrapper punched back, hitting the guy right on the nose.

The two went at it, punching and kicking. Players from both benches rushed out and pulled them apart.

The umpire ran over and pointed at Scrapper.

"Out of the game!"

Scrapper roared. *"Me? He* threw the first punch! I was minding my own business! What are you throwing me out for?"

"You interfered with the play," the ump answered. Then he turned around and signaled that the batter was out.

Now Coach Cunningham came roaring out of the dugout. He ran over to the umpire and got right into his face.

"Whatta ya mean, out? That was a foul ball! He dropped it! My player didn't have a chance to get out of his way! What do you mean, out?"

The umpire snarled back. "Do you want me to spell it for you?"

"Yeah!"

"O-U-T!"

"You're nuts!" Cunningham yelled back. "Do you want me to spell *that* for you?"

Scrapper joined in. "You can't throw me out for just standing there!"

"I just did!" the ump shot back.

"He hit my player!" Cunningham shouted. And then he jabbed his finger into the umpire's chest protector. That was it. The ump pumped his arm, like he was hitchhiking an airplane.

"You're outta here!" he cried to Cunningham. "Both of you! Off the field! Now!"

There was nothing more to say. And Cunningham knew it. He had been thrown out enough times in his career to know when it was over. Scrapper was still jumping all over the place. Cunningham grabbed him by the shoulder.

"Forget it," he said. "Pack it in."

As the other players headed back for the dugout, Scrapper reached down and picked up the ball.

"Hey," he called out to the catcher. "Did you forget something?" He tossed the ball to the catcher.

Heading down the runway, Coach Cunningham noticed that his second baseman was limping.

"I told you you should have stayed out of the game."

Scrapper shrugged it away. "Aw . . . old war wound, that's all."

As they got to the locker room, Cunningham chuckled.

"Your first major-league toss, Mitchell. I guess that's something to write home about."

Scrapper didn't answer. What he was thinking was, *Not if you know my father.*

Fourteen years in the major leagues and Joe Mitchell had never once been ejected from a game.

The White Sox were in the middle of a road trip that was taking them all over the state. Scrapper got a chance to go to Disney World and spend his money on rides and food. The place was incredible. The rides were like nothing he had ever been on before. Even Epcot Center was kind of fun.

On another day off, Scrapper and some of the other players took a trip to Cape Canaveral to see where the Shuttle took off. When the tour guide found out that some of the Chicago White Sox were taking the tour, she sent them along to an official of the Cape who gave them the "inside" tour. The guys even met one of the astronauts who had been up in space. The astronaut admitted he was a Dodgers fan.

Before they left, Scrapper promised the astronaut that if he was ever in Chicago, Scrapper would get him some free tickets to a game.

"That's *if* you're on the team," one of the other guys reminded him.

"No problem."

Except for all the cuts and bruises, Scrapper was having an excellent spring. Scrapper's brand of hustle was impressing the coaches. For a short player, Scrapper had incredible range in the field. He plugged up holes that other infielders might have had trouble with. Scrapper was everywhere at once. Diving to his left. Scrambling to his right. It was a common sight to see Scrapper rising up on his knees to throw off balance to first and nail the runner. He was nonstop.

It was also becoming a common sight to see the other infielders grumbling about the rookie second baseman. The problem was, Scrapper's "range" was sometimes taking him a little *too* far. Bounding balls to the shortstop side of the bag would suddenly be swallowed up by Scrapper, instead of by the shortstop. And times when Scrapper should have been flipping the ball to Jimmy Masters to turn the double play, he was holding on to it instead and making the play all by himself.

"Why don't they just send us all down to the minors and let Mitchell go up to Chicago all by himself?" Masters was heard saying in the locker room after one of the games. "He already thinks he's a one-man team."

Scrapper knew that some of the guys were grumbling about his attitude. But he figured that was their problem, not his. Why shouldn't he play the best and hardest that he could?

It was in a game against Kansas City that the problem really got out of hand. The White Sox were being clobbered. No one was doing anything right. It was the Kansas City's half of the seventh. Two out, and a man on first. The guy on first had been taking a huge lead. It didn't take a fortune-teller to predict that he was going to try to steal. Scrapper kept yelling in to the pitcher to keep an eye on the runner.

"Come on!" he was yelling, "we don't want to lose him!"

On a two-two pitch, the runner took off. Scrapper ran to the bag to take the throw from the catcher. It came in on the money. But halfway down to second, the runner had slipped and almost fallen down. Scrapper got the throw and took off down the base path after the runner, pumping his arm like he was going to throw the ball to the White Sox first baseman, who was coming in for the rundown. The runner didn't know which way to go.

"Throw it!" the first baseman yelled to Scrapper. "Throw it!"

But Scrapper held on to the ball. He barreled down after the runner and lunged for him . . . and just missed him. The runner jumped away from the tag and headed for second. Scrapper turned and charged after the guy. Jimmy Masters had moved in from short, and was waving his glove for the ball. But Scrapper ignored him, too, and dove for the runner. He caught him around the ankle. The two of them tumbled to the ground. Scrapper held up his glove to show the umpire that he still had the ball.

"Out!"

As Scrapper trotted into the dugout, the shortstop and the first baseman closed in on him.

"What's the big idea!" the first baseman shouted.

Masters picked it up. "This is a team, Mitchell, not a hot-dog stand!"

"Hey," Scrapper yelled back. "I got him out!"

"And what was I doing?" Masters asked. "Standing around with my hands in my pockets? You're supposed to throw the ball on a rundown, not hog it!"

They had reached the dugout. Scrapper went for a drink of water, but the two guys stayed on him.

"If you want to run around tackling people, why don't you play football?"

That was it. Scrapper spun around and faced them.

"Maybe if some of you guys played a little harder we wouldn't be getting whipped like this in the first place! I'm the only guy out there even breaking a sweat!"

"You think you're playing harder than the rest of us?"

"I don't think it. I *know* it!"

Coach Cunningham called out from the dugout steps.

"You want to hear what I know, Mitchell? I know we're waiting for you to get out there and bat! Come on, you're up!"

Scrapper grabbed his bat and hurried out to home plate, slicing the bat in the air. *I'll show them*, he thought.

Three pitches later he was heading back for the dugout, ready to kill the first person who opened their mouth. But the first person who said anything to him was Coach Cunningham.

"What's the problem there, Mitchell?" the coach said, half smiling. "I didn't even see you break a sweat."

By the end of the road trip, the White Sox were really coming together. They had the pitching, they had the hitting. A lot of depth. The only weak spot was their defense. There were just too many errors. Too many shabby plays in the field.

"You guys aren't consistent," Coach Cunningham complained one afternoon during a practice.

"In one game you're brilliant. In the next game, you stink. We're not going to get any pennants that way. Fundamentals. I want you guys fielding grounders in your sleep!"

The final game of the road trip was against the Phillies. Scrapper was more keyed up than usual. This was his dad's old team. The Phillies had retired Joe Mitchell's number when he quit baseball. They had held Joe Mitchell Day at Three River Stadium. That was one of the proudest days of Scrapper's life. It was also the only time he had ever seen tears in his father's eyes. That was something Scrapper would never forget.

It felt strange for Scrapper when he got to the ball park. A couple of the Phillies coaches had played with Joe Mitchell, and they remembered his son as being half as tall and twice as light. A few of them came up to Scrapper during batting practice. They wanted to know how his father was doing. Each of them also told Scrapper what he already knew and what he had already heard a thousand times before.

"Your father was the best." "They just don't make them like Joe anymore. One of a kind."

While he was taking his practice swings in the cage, Scrapper overheard two of the Phillies old-timers talking.

"They say he's pretty feisty in the field."

"Sure, but how's his bat? You remember how Joe used to clobber them."

"It's pretty average, I think.

"Too bad. The White Sox need another second baseman like they need a hole in the head."

The ball came in and Scrapper creamed it. He wasn't thinking. Instinctively, he took off running for first, only to remember that this was just batting practice. He felt his ears turning red as he came back and picked up his bat. The two Phillies coaches were chuckling. Scrapper knew exactly what they were thinking.

Scrapper was even more verbal than usual when the White Sox took the field. He wanted more than anything to beat the Phillies.

It was a good game. The players on both teams were in a groove. Except the pitchers. They were getting shelled. The ball was dropping in everywhere.

One bat on the White Sox was silent. Scrapper's. In his first three at bats he popped out to short, hit the ball right to the first baseman, and struck out. Things weren't much better for him in the field. It wasn't that he was playing badly, just that the ball wasn't coming to him.

It took Scrapper a few innings before he figured it out. And then he got it. He was being frozen out. A couple of times, Masters waved him off the double play and turned it—or tried to—himself. It was the kind of move Scrapper usually made. And when Scrapper was playing cutoff, the outfielders were throwing the ball right past him. By the sixth inning, Scrapper had actually touched the ball only twice. It was no Golden Glove outing, that was for sure.

In the top of the eighth, Scrapper drew a two-out walk. He didn't walk down to first. He ran.

This is it, he told himself. *My last chance to get into the game.*

"Now you stay put," the first-base coach muttered to him when he got there. With two out, the last thing the White Sox wanted was to risk a steal.

Scrapper was off on the next pitch. He charged down to second and dove into the bag. It was such a surprise, the catcher hadn't even thrown the ball.

Scrapper got up and dusted himself off. He glanced over at the third-base coach, who was shaking his head. No.

The pitcher set, checked Scrapper at second, then threw the pitch.

Scrapper was off again. He could see the guys in the dugout jump to their feet. This time the catcher whipped the ball down to third, but Scrapper executed a perfect hook slide and avoided the tag.

The players in the White Sox dugout were going nuts. The third-base coach was clapping his hands, but he was also frowning at the same time. He called time while Scrapper was dusting himself off.

"Enough's enough," the coach muttered to Scrapper. "If you dare try to steal home without my say-so, I'll fine you."

Scrapper was already up on his toes. "How much?" he asked.

The coach just shook his head. "Don't even ask."

Scrapper didn't have to. The batter sent the

next pitch into the corner for a single. Scrapper trotted down to home plate like he had all the time in the world. He almost could have walked.

It wasn't until he touched the plate and looked up into the stands that Scrapper saw his father. Joe Mitchell was sitting there, behind the Phillies dugout, munching on a hot dog. He waved at his son and gave him the thumbs-up.

Scrapper turned around quickly and hustled back to the dugout. Some of the guys met him there and pounded him on the back for his good hustle. Scrapper didn't even see them. His mind was racing.

What is he doing here?

NINE

The competition to make the Dodgers pitching staff was pretty fierce. Even as good as he was pitching, Magic figured it was still a long shot. There were plenty of good veteran right-handed starters on the staff already. Magic didn't even want to think about the bullpen. He was a starter, not a reliever. He couldn't imagine being sent out to the bullpen. That was like being sent to Siberia.

What bothered Magic even more than the idea of being sent to the bullpen was a dream he had been having lately, over and over. Actually, it was a nightmare. In it, he was pitching in the seventh game of the World Series. It was the ninth inning. The score was tied, and the bases were loaded. The stadium in the dream was three times bigger than any regular stadium. It was huge! The upper deck was so high that the fans up in the bleachers were sitting in the clouds. Magic would wind up and pitch. And as the ball sailed in toward the waiting batter, it got bigger and bigger and bigger. By the time it got to the batter, the ball was the about the size of a beach ball. The batter couldn't miss it! The batter would shift his feet, and start to swing—

That was where Magic always woke up. Right before the batter creamed the ball. Sometimes Magic was covered in sweat. The dream seemed so real, it usually took Magic an hour or so to fall back asleep. Another thing about the dream . . . his family was always sitting there, right behind home plate, keeping their fingers crossed.

Magic didn't tell anyone about the dream. They would have said he was nuts. After all, he was the spring sensation. Magic's split-fingered fastball was practically unhittable. His change-up had batters swinging at the ball before it even got to the plate.

Still, Magic worried. Ben Porter, the Dodger catcher, just laughed at him.

"You're supposed to worry when you're pitching *lousy*, not when you're striking out every batter in sight!"

But Magic could only think about that dream. It must be a bad-luck omen, he thought.

Every time Magic got out on the mound, he crossed his fingers before the first pitch. He also kept a pair of dice in his pocket. His lucky dice. Magic's sister, Maria, had given them to him just before he left for Florida. She got them from the family's Monopoly game. Before each game, Magic stayed in the locker room and rolled the dice over and over until he finally rolled a nine. That was Magic's lucky number. Nine good innings. That's all he asked.

The Orioles were in for a pair of games. Magic was scheduled to pitch the second game. During the first game, it was his job to watch the Orioles' pitcher and mark down on a chart what kinds of pitches he was throwing.

Magic had just suited up and was looking around the training room for the pitching chart when the pitching coach came running in, all out of breath.

"Ramirez. Good, you're dressed. Get warmed up. You're pitching today."

"No, I'm not," Magic said. "I'm pitching tomorrow. Hartman's pitching today."

The coach was shaking his head.

"Hartman's done something to his shoulder. It's swollen up. He can't pitch. We've got to change the rotation. You're in. Come on. You'd better get out there and warm up."

"But I—"

"Let's go!"

Magic went to his locker to get his glove. He looked up on the shelf for his lucky dice, but then remembered that they were still in his travel bag back at the motel.

Ramirez had hoped to get a good look at the Baltimore hitters today before facing them tomorrow. He didn't really know the book on them.

"Just throw what I tell you," Ben Porter said to him after the warm-up. "I know these guys. Don't worry."

Don't worry. Right.

The first batter Magic faced wore the number nine. *Figures*, Magic thought. Porter called for a low ball at the knees. Magic rocked and fired. The ball stayed up and hit the outside corner for a strike.

"Lucky," Magic muttered to himself. Just lucky.

The catcher wanted a curve next, trailing out. *No problem*, thought Magic as he went into his motion. His curve had felt good during warm-up.

The ball went right down the center of the plate. The batter swung and missed. Strike two.

Now Porter was confused. He looked at the ball, and then handed it to the umpire. The ump inspected it, then tossed it back out to Magic.

But if the catcher was confused, it was nothing compared to the pitcher. Even though his first two pitches had been strikes, they hadn't gone anywhere near where they were supposed to go. Magic had no control.

Number nine dug in and waited for the next pitch. Porter signaled for heat. He wanted the fastball. Right down the middle. Magic set and threw.

He felt like he was back in that dream. The ball had nothing on it. It wasn't even a fastball; it was almost a change-up. It floated in to the plate just like a Frisbee. The batter cut at it too early and missed. He was out on three pitches. Over in the dugout, the Dodgers cheered. As the next batter stood in, Porter came out to the mound.

"What's the idea?" he snapped. "You're supposed to fool the batter, not me!"

"Sorry," Magic said. "The ball just got away from me."

"I'll say. It almost got away from me! Settle down now. This next guy is a low-ball hitter. So keep everything up around the letters. Got it?"

Magic nodded. The catcher dropped the ball into Magic's glove and went back to the plate. Magic pulled off his glove and warmed up the ball, rubbing it between his hands. It looked like he was winding a clock. *Concentrate*, he was thinking. *Concentrate.*

Porter squatted behind the plate and gave Magic the target. High. Magic set and fired. The ball came in low. The guy crushed it. Home run.

Magic had problems with his control for the next three innings. The Orioles batters chipped away at him for six hits and three runs. Magic was finally pulled in the fourth. It was his worst outing of the spring.

Back in the locker room, Magic sat on the bench in front of his locker for half an hour without moving. He thought about his buddies, Scrapper and Green. What if they made it into the big leagues and he didn't? He thought about his family and how excited they were for him. Magic was glad none of them had seen *this* game.

If only Hartman hadn't hurt his shoulder. If only Magic had pitched tomorrow's game, like he was supposed to.

Forget it, Magic told himself at last. *You're going to "if" yourself until you're crazy.*

He finally grabbed his towel and headed off for the showers. He didn't see the bar of soap that someone had left on the floor. He turned on the shower water and set the temperature. *Everyone has a bad day,* he was telling himself. *Just forget it.*

He got under the water, and a second later it went completely hot. The showers were really lousy down here. Magic jumped back, and landed right on the bar of soap. His arms flew in the air as he tried to keep his balance, but . . . *crash!* He went flying to the floor and landed on his right shoulder.

It took a few seconds for the pain to hit him. When it did, he had to grit his teeth to keep from crying out. The pain shot up and down his arm and into his back.

Magic got back up to his feet and angrily kicked the bar of soap clean out of the shower. He went to adjust the water, and realized he couldn't lift his arm without the pain shooting through it. He tried several times, but each time the arm felt like it was on fire.

It was hard to get dressed. Magic was glad that the game was still going on and there was no one in the locker room to see him.

By that night, the shoulder was swollen. Magic got a bucket of ice from the motel's ice machine and kept the ice on his shoulder until he went to bed. In the morning, the swelling was down, and he could move his arm again. *Whew*, he thought. *Close call.*

Because he had pitched the day before, Magic wouldn't have to use his arm at all today. He was glad for the chance to rest it. He volunteered to chart the pitches that afternoon. The Dodgers won. Magic didn't bother telling anyone about the arm. He could tough it out.

But the arm stayed sore. Magic took it easy during practice the next couple of days. No need to push it. He was scheduled to pitch against Atlanta on Friday. Magic was psyched to show the team that his four innings against the Orioles had just been a fluke.

Magic pitched okay for the first four innings against Atlanta. It wasn't really his best stuff, but he was keeping the game close. Still, he was throwing a lot of pitches, running up a lot of full counts. He could feel the shoulder beginning to get stiff.

In the fifth inning, Magic ran the count to three and two on the lead-off batter. The guy fouled off the next four pitches. *Great*, thought Magic. *The guy's going to pull a Scrapper on me. I'll be out here all day.*

The shoulder had begun to throb by now. Magic could feel it affecting his pitches. He leaned in for the sign. His catcher wanted a slider. Magic shook him off. Magic wanted to throw the fastball. Even if it hurt his arm, it was still his best pitch. He just wanted to get this guy out. Porter caught on. He called for the split-fingered fastball. Magic kicked and fired.

The ball almost took the batter's head off. It flew in at ninety-two miles an hour, right for the guy's head.

"Look out!" Magic yelled.

The batter spun to get out of the way, but the ball caught him right in the side of the batter's helmet. He went down.

Magic rushed in to the plate. He had never hit a batter before. Never. But the batter was all right. Shakily, he got to his feet, glaring at Magic.

"You trying to kill me?" he yelled.

Magic opened his mouth, but nothing came out. The umpire moved around quickly in front of the batter and told him to take his base. It wasn't until he headed off for first base that Magic saw the number on the back of his jersey. Nine.

Magic was rattled. Back on the mound he tried to concentrate on the next batter. But his first pitch went way wide, right past the catcher's glove. Wild pitch. The runner advanced to second. Magic couldn't believe it. *At this rate,* he thought, *I might as well pitch left handed. Or with my eyes closed. I couldn't do much worse.*

Magic picked up the rosin bag and bounced it around in his hand. The runner on second was taking a pretty good lead. Magic spun and tried to pick him off. Instead, he almost picked off the second baseman, who was running in to take the throw. The ball bounced off the second baseman's leg and rolled onto the outfield grass. The runner hoofed it to third. There wasn't even a throw.

This was nuts. Magic thought, *My* dog *can throw better than this!* He saw Coach McGreevey, the pitching coach, in the dugout, talking with Lasorda. This was *worse* than the dream.

Magic turned his attention back to the batter. He went into his windup and threw. The batter connected and hit a high fly to deep center. The runner tagged up at third and scored easily.

Magic finally pitched his way out of the inning. But his control was terrible. His shoulder throbbed with each pitch. He was pulled in the fifth, after walking a batter. The pitching coach walked with him back to the locker room.

"Don't sweat it, Robo-Arm. We'll get you straightened out."

When Magic went in for his shower, he spotted a bar of soap on the floor. He went over to it and kicked it as hard as he could.

"This is your fault!" he yelled.

Great, he thought. *I'm talking to the soap now.* He turned on the shower water.

The next day, Magic found out what it was the coach had in mind. Magic was being assigned to the bullpen. A reliever. He was as good as off the team.

"Just get a few saves under your belt," the bullpen coach told him. "You'll be back in the rotation in no time."

But by the end of the week, Magic had gone in as a reliever four times. He had only gotten a total of one save.

You'll be back in the rotation in no time.

Yeah, thought Magic as the team boarded the bus for Winter Haven. *Like, never.*

TEN

Scrapper sat across the table from his father, pushing his food around with his fork. It was a pretty fancy restaurant that his father had picked out. Every time Scrapper took a sip from his water glass, a guy in a tuxedo hurried over and filled the glass back up.

"What's wrong, Glen?" Joe Mitchell asked. "I've never seen you not eat."

Joe Mitchell was almost finished with his steak. He was a big man. He could have eaten the whole cow and still had room for dessert.

Scrapper just didn't feel like eating right now. He tried to joke it off.

"I guess I've been eating too much fast food lately," he said. "I've forgotten how to use one of these."

Joe Mitchell laughed. "Well, you see, that's

called a fork, and what you do, is you poke it into your steak, like this, and you—"

Scrapper cut him off. "I know, I know. I was just kidding."

Joe Mitchell sat back in his chair. He could see that something was bothering his son.

"So was I," he said.

Scrapper was looking down at his plate.

"Yeah. Well . . ."

"Do you want to tell me about it?" Joe Mitchell said.

"Tell you about what?"

"About whatever it is that's bugging you. You've hardly said a word since I got down here. And that's sure not like you."

Scrapper cut off a big piece of steak and stuck it in his mouth.

"I can't talk with my mouth full," he said, chewing.

Scrapper felt rotten. Here his dad had come all the way to Florida to surprise him, and Scrapper could barely talk to him. And this restaurant where they were eating wasn't just your average feed bag, either. Scrapper knew his dad was dropping a bundle on this dinner. The food was so expensive they didn't even put the prices on the menu. Scrapper figured they probably didn't want people to have a heart attack until *after* they'd eaten.

"You showed good hustle out there on the bases today," Joe Mitchell said. "That impresses the coaches."

Scrapper swallowed his piece of steak. "They chewed me out," he said.

"Chewed you out?"

"Yeah. They said I could've been thrown out and killed the inning."

"But you weren't. You scored."

Scrapper poked his fork into another piece of steak. It *was* good steak. "Yeah, tell *them* about it."

Joe Mitchell thought for a moment. "Maybe I will," he said.

Scrapper blurted out, "*No!*"

He was loud, a couple of people at the other tables turned to look at him. A man with a small moustache pointed to Joe Mitchell and whispered something to his wife.

"Hey, now," Scrapper's dad said. "What's the problem here? I just said I might have a word with your coach."

"You can't do that!" Scrapper said. "I'll be mud, Dad. Do you know what they called me when I first got down here?"

"What?"

"'Junior'. They called me Junior. As in Joe junior."

Joe Mitchell smiled. "I should be proud of that."

"But how about me? It drives me crazy. I'm not you!"

"No, you're not me," Joe said calmly. "And you shouldn't have to pretend you are."

"I'm not pretending I'm you," Scrapper said. "But every time I turn around, somebody's always comparing me to you!"

"Come on now, son. We've been through this before."

Scrapper didn't say anything. He took another

bite of steak, then pushed his plate to the side. A waiter was right there to scoop it up. Scrapper glared at him. He looked over and saw that the man with the small moustache was coming their way.

"Don't look now," Scrapper said to his dad. "But here comes your fan club."

The man came up to the table and cleared his throat.

"Excuse me. But . . . aren't you Joe Mitchell?"

Scrapper rolled his eyes. "No," he said. "He's the Easter Bunny."

Joe Mitchell glared across the table at Scrapper.

"Glen!" he snapped.

"Sorry," Scrapper mumbled. But what he was thinking was, *And I'm Easter Bunny Junior.*

When Scrapper arrived at the ball park the next day, his teammates practically mobbed him.

"Where's your dad?"

"Is he coming to the game today?"

"Come on, Mitchell. Where are you hiding him?"

Scrapper pushed his way past them to get to his locker. The other players looked at him like he was crazy. Jimmy Masters was standing at Scrapper's locker, waiting for him.

"What's the deal, Mitchell? Do we have to watch you again today? We want to see the *real* ballplayer in your family."

That was it. Scrapper jumped on him and the two fell to the floor, kicking and hitting. The others crowded around in a circle. A few tried to pull them apart, but they were going at it too hard. Especially Scrapper.

"Hey! What's this?"

Coach Cunningham fought his way through the crowd. When he saw what was going on he boomed out, *"Cut it! Now!"*

They did. Scrapper and Masters broke apart and sat there on the floor, panting. Coach Cunningham glared down at them.

"You two!" he said angrily. "Don't even suit up. You're suspended!"

Scrapper leaped to his feet. "What?"

"You heard me. You're not playing today, Mitchell. And one more word out of you and you won't play tomorrow, either! If you want to see the game today, buy a ticket!"

The coach stormed off. For a minute, no one said anything. Finally, the other players drifted off to their lockers and started getting on their uniforms. Scrapper and Masters just stood there like a pair of statues. Masters turned to Scrapper.

"We really blew it."

Scrapper nodded his head. He was still too stunned to speak. Suspended! How was he going to tell his dad that he had come all the way down here to watch his son *not* play? This was the worst thing that could have possibly happened.

"Come on," Masters said. "We'd better get out of here."

Scrapper followed him out of the locker room. Outside, Masters turned to him.

"Hey, Mitch. I'm sorry about that."

Scrapper finally found his voice. "No, *I'm* sorry

about it. Man, I'm cooked for sure. My dad came all the way down here to see me play."

"What are you going to do?"

Scrapper gave a weak laugh. "Join the Army."

Scrapper hung around the parking lot until the game started. He didn't know what to do. He could hear the crowd making a lot of noise. It sounded like it must be a good game. And here he was, walking back and forth among the cars.

Finally, Scrapper went in. It was the fifth inning. Scrapper couldn't believe the score. The White Sox were eating the other team alive. They were already ahead eight to nothing. Scrapper groaned. The team was hot, and here he was in the stands.

Scrapper saw his father sitting down near the White Sox dugout. Scrapper bought two hot dogs and headed down. His father looked up.

"Oh, there you are."

Scrapper handed him a hot dog and sat down next to him. He couldn't think of anything to say. Joe Mitchell took a bite out of his hot dog.

"Good game," he said. "Your guys are killing them."

Scrapper said nothing. *My guys*, he thought. *That's a joke. Another few weeks and "my guys" will be opening up the season in Chicago, and I'll be back there looking for a job.* He wondered what else he could do for a living. *How about shoes?* he thought bitterly. *Everybody needs shoes. Maybe I'll just sell shoes.*

He felt terrible. He wished his father would say something about why he wasn't playing. But Joe

Mitchell was just acting like there was nothing wrong at all. He was into the game.

"This kid's got real potential, doesn't he?" Scrapper's dad said at one point. Scrapper looked up to see who he was talking about. Chris Wilson was stepping into the box.

"He's all right," Scrapper said.

"All right? He seems to have a pretty good bat."

Scrapper looked over at the scoreboard, where Wilson's average was being flashed.

"Heck, mine's better than that," he said.

Joe Mitchell didn't answer right away. The pitch came in to Wilson. He fouled it off.

"That may be," Joe Mitchell said. "But *he's* in the game, isn't he?"

Scrapper slowly looked up at his father. "You noticed, huh?"

Joe Mitchell said nothing.

After the game, Scrapper took his father down to the White Sox locker room. It felt strange, standing there in his regular clothes while the other guys were streaming in all sweaty in their uniforms. Scrapper was jealous. He cleared his throat.

"Hey, guys. I . . . uh. This is my . . . This is Joe Mitchell."

The players came in on him like a big wave. Scrapper backed away and stood off by his locker, watching. His dad loved it. Some of the rookies were actually asking for his autograph. Chris Wilson was one of them. The guys were peppering Joe Mitchell with questions about his days as a Phillie, about his thirty-home-run seasons, his eight consecutive All Star Games, his World Series grand slam. . . .

Scrapper leaned against his locker and listened. The truth was, Scrapper never got tired of hearing his dad's stories. His dad was the greatest; it was as simple as that. Scrapper figured that if he managed to achieve even half the things that his father had during his career, that would be pretty good. But it wouldn't be *great*. And Scrapper wanted to be great. He and Magic and old DT Green . . . they had promised each other way back in high school that they were all going to be great.

Sure, Scrapper said to himself. *What am I going to brag about when I'm Dad's age? About the day I got thrown out of a game before the game even started? Great.*

Joe Mitchell flew back to Chicago that night. Scrapper went with him out to the airport. Scrapper didn't say much. He didn't have to. His dad was still talking about the good old days. Once Joe Mitchell got rolling, he was like a machine you couldn't turn off.

Just before he got on the plane, Scrapper's dad said, "So, your mother and I want good seats for opening day."

Scrapper just shrugged. "Yeah," he said. "So do I."

The White Sox were heading into the final week of spring training. Their last game was next Saturday against the Red Sox. Sox versus Sox. Several cuts had been made over the past weeks, but there were more to come. Only twenty-five players could be on the roster when the team flew to Chicago. A few more players would have to go. This last week would be crucial.

Scrapper couldn't have picked a worse time to slump. It wasn't that he wasn't trying. He was doing that. Scrapper was diving for the grounders. He was charging in on the bunt. He was keeping the pepper going. And he was even much more of a team player now. He was no longer hot-dogging the double-play ball or charging in on other people's plays.

But the ball was just taking funny bounces, and was squirting between his legs. Scrapper was misjudging easy grounders. He was bobbling the ball and he was rushing his throw to first. In a game against the Yankees, Scrapper's rocket to first went right into the Yankee dugout and smashed the water cooler. Water ran everywhere. Meanwhile, the go-ahead run scored. The Yankees ended up winning.

Scrapper began to wonder seriously about that new career selling shoes. At this rate, he told himself, he'd probably even mess *that* up!

Mitchell wasn't having much better luck at the plate. He tried changing his stance, but that didn't help. He took extra batting practice, but everything he hit still found its way right into someone's glove. Nothing helped. Scrapper went hitless in four straight games. The one time he did draw a walk, Scrapper played cat and mouse with the pitcher and was picked off base.

The dugout seemed awfully quiet when he got

back to it. Scrapper took off his cap and threw it against the back wall. Chris Wilson came up to him.

"You're pushing too hard," he said.

Scrapper snapped back. "There's no such thing!"

But there was. And Scrapper was doing it. Ever since his father's visit, Scrapper's playing had gone downhill. He was playing extra hard, as if he could somehow make up for that game that he had missed.

"It's a slump, kid," Coach Cunningham said to him after the Yankees loss. "Everybody has them."

Scrapper just mumbled. He didn't have time to stand around and talk about his slump. The final game was two days away. Scrapper had work to do. He had the pitching machine in his arms and was heading back out onto the field.

Hours later, the sun was almost down. The stadium was empty, except for Scrapper, standing at home plate. The only sounds in the ball park were the *click-whoosh* of the pitching machine, and the *crack* of Scrapper's bat against the ball. The outfield looked like a field of cotton. Hundreds of baseballs were scattered everywhere.

Scrapper choked up on the bat and bent over the plate. *Red Sox*, he thought. *Two days.*

Click-whoosh! Crack!

Another baseball fell into the outfield.

ELEVEN

As the Dodgers bus pulled up to the ball park in Winter Haven, the players were a little quieter than usual. The team was scheduled to play their last game of the spring-training season against the Red Sox. This was it. After today's game, the final cut was going to be made. The roster would be firmed up. For the luckiest of the players, that would mean Opening Day in another week; the TV cameras, the pregame interviews. . . . For some of the others, it would mean Triple A, just one step away from the majors. Anything less . . . nobody even wanted to think about that.

The last person off the bus was Magic Ramirez. Magic had his travel bag slung over his shoulder and he was wearing his new aviator sunglasses. He stopped on the bottom step of the bus and looked off toward the ball park. In his pocket, his hand was fumbling with his pair of good-luck dice. For the first time in a long time, he felt lucky again.

Magic was slated to pitch the final game. Just as the coach had said, after a few games as a reliever, he'd gotten out of the bullpen. Now he was back as a starter!

It was a perfect day for a ball game. A storm had passed through a few days before and left behind temperatures in the mid-seventies. There was a slight, warm breeze on the field and a clear blue sky above. Pitcher's weather.

After Magic's warm-up tosses, the Dodgers' pitching coach pulled Magic to the side.

"If that shoulder starts acting up, you tell me," he said.

Magic nodded his head. *It'd have to be broken before I pulled myself*, he thought. His entire career was riding on this game. This last week and a half of bullpen duty had been pure torture. His pitching had remained shaky the entire time. A couple of times, his inside pitches had gotten away from him, and he had almost beaned a couple of batters. It had him nervous.

But now he was being given the nod to start the final game. Magic had no idea how his arm was going to behave. He did know one thing, though. If he hit another batter with a pitch, he'd quit. He'd call home and tell his father that he just wasn't cut out for the majors. He'd apply to college.

Magic was going through his own warm-up

routine on the sidelines when he spotted Dave Green over in the batting cage, loosening up. As soon as Green was finished, Magic hustled over to him.

"Hey, Rubber Bat!" he called out. Green turned and broke into a huge smile. They high-fived each other.

"Well, if it isn't the only pitcher around I have any trouble with!" Green said.

Magic laughed. "Still humble, eh?"

"I call 'em like I see 'em, man."

They both laughed.

"How's it going?" Magic said seriously. "Last couple of weeks have been bad for me."

"Tell me about it," Green said. "I'm surprised they haven't demoted me to bat boy by now."

"What, you, too?"

"You'd better believe it," Green said. "I'm hitting the ball fine. That's not the problem. It's this coach we've got. He just won't let up on me, Magic. It's been driving me nuts."

"What's the problem?"

Green pushed his cap back on his head and scratched his head. "Catch this," he said. "The coach says my ego is as big as my batting average."

"What are you hitting these days?"

"About three forty-six."

"Man! That's some ego!"

The two of them laughed again.

"You heard anything about Scrap?" Magic asked.

"The White Sox are due down tomorrow. Last game. I can't wait."

Magic made a gangster's face and cracked his knuckles, one at a time. "Well, you gotta get through the game first, buster."

Green laughed. "No sweat."

Magic added, "And don't even *try* to hit my first pitch, hotshot. I'm going to blow it right by you."

Green frowned. "I don't know if I'm playing yet."

"Of course, you're playing!" Magic said. "A guy with a three-forty-six ego?"

Green shook his head. "That's just it. The coach has been playing around with the lineup a lot this last week. Some days I'm in, some days I'm keeping the bench warm."

Magic couldn't believe it.

Green shrugged. "Big leagues. What can I say? Look, I'd better go check on the lineup." He started back toward the dugout, then stopped and turned back around. A huge sarcastic smile was on his face.

"Hey, Magic," Green said. "Good luck."

Magic made a face like he had been shot. He pointed a finger at his friend. "Doomed," he said. "If you do get up to bat . . . you're dead."

Green gave him a thumbs-up, then trotted back to his dugout. It was great seeing old Magic again. It was like old times. He chuckled to himself. *Old times? Heck, I'm too young to have old times already.*

Green hopped down into the dugout. Suddenly

he felt great. Pete Kenney was standing there, adjusting the strap on his sunglasses.

"Hey, Pete," Green said. "Your shoes are untied."

It was the oldest trick in the book, but Kenney fell for it. He looked down, and Green flipped him on the nose.

"Gotcha."

"Oh, real cute, Shorty," Kenney said. "Real cute."

Green headed down to the other end of the dugout. The lineup was posted on the far wall. Green ran his finger down the names. His great mood dropped right away. His name wasn't on the list.

"What's wrong?" Kenney asked as he came over.

Green pushed past him and headed for the runway.

"Nothing," he grunted. "My shoes are untied, that's all."

Magic was hot. More that that, he was pumped up like never before. He couldn't keep still up on the mound. The moment he got the ball back from the catcher, he would come down off the back of the mound, pick up the rosin bag, drop it, screw the ball into the palm of his hand, tug on the brim of his cap, check the outfield, squint up at the sun, and then charge back up onto the rubber.

"You ever seen him like this?" Lasorda asked

the pitching coach. "I've never seen him so keyed up."

The pitching coach shook his head slowly. "Nope. Never have."

Lasorda jammed his fingers into his back pockets. "Well, I like it," he said. "I wanna see more of it."

He cupped his hand to his mouth and yelled out some instructions to his outfielders. He wanted them to shift over for the next batter, who was a pull hitter. The pitching coach told him to save his breath.

"Why?" Lasorda was red in the face from yelling.

The pitching coach just signaled for him to keep on the mound. Four pitches later, the batter was out.

"All right!" Lasorda yelled out, clapping his hands. "Keep it going!"

Up on the mound, his pitcher was roaming around like an angry bear. He picked up the rosin bag, looked up at the sky, rubbed down the ball . . .

Over in the Red Sox dugout, Green sat back on the bench, halfway enjoying the show. He always knew that his friend was a great pitcher. But he had never seen him pitching like *this* before! The way Magic was putting the Red Sox batters down one after another, Green was almost glad he wasn't in the lineup.

Almost.

Magic got the final out of the inning on a strikeout. He jogged quickly into the dugout and dropped onto the bench. He looked out at the scoreboard. For the Red Sox, there were nothing but zeroes in every column. Six innings now. Magic looked away quickly. He had to concentrate. It was bad luck to stare at the scoreboard.

It was clear that nobody better talk to Magic while he sat on the bench waiting to go back out and pitch. He was pitching the game of his life. Talk was distracting. While his team took its turn at the plate, Magic sat quietly on the bench, looking out at the row of palm trees that ran along the back fence of the park. He didn't even watch his teammates. He didn't see the back-to-back home runs. He didn't even hear the coach screaming out at the batters and yelling out at the umpires. All Magic saw was the row of palm trees blowing in the spring breeze.

Back out on the mound the next inning, Magic allowed a lead-off walk, but he got the next batter to hit into a double play. The next batter due up was the Red Sox's left fielder, Pete Kenney. But before Kenney had gotten into the batter's box, he was called back to the dugout. Magic kicked at the dirt around the rubber as he waited for the pinch hitter to be announced. He felt fine. He had all the time in the world.

The announcement came over the PA system. "Attention. Now batting for Pete Kenney. Number seven. David Green."

Magic snapped to attention. Green was coming out to the plate, swinging a pair of bats. As he got to the batter's box, he tossed one of the bats away.

He stepped in and took a few swings, then he held his hand up.

"Time!" the Red Sox coach called out.

Green backed out of the box and adjusted his batting glove, tugging it tighter. He glanced over his shoulder at his third-base coach, who was flashing every signal in the book. Green nodded. He looked out toward the mound, whipped his bat in the air, then stepped carefully back into the box. The catcher settled in and called for a curve.

Magic threw. The ball sailed in toward Green's knees, then tailed off over the plate. Green stayed with it. He swung and got a piece of it, and sent the ball flying out toward right field. The crowd started to rise . . . but the ball drifted just foul. Another few inches, and it would have been gone.

Green choked up on the bat and waited for the next pitch. Coach Brooks's words were still buzzing in his ears. "Green, you're in. If anybody can hit this guy, it's you." Green knew that this was his big chance. The way things had been going lately, it might even be his last chance.

The next pitch that came in was alive. Magic's knuckler. Green held back and took it for a ball. It seemed to Green that Magic had taken some of the stuff off that last pitch. Maybe the long foul had rattled him. When the next pitch came in, Green knew it for sure. The pitch was high and away. Suddenly Green knew what he had to do.

"Hey!" Green called out toward the mound. "You think I'm chasing butterflies here? Come on! Let's have a *real* pitch!"

Magic glared at him. He kicked and fired. The pitch came in wide.

Green called out, "Looking good, Roberto! Reeeeal good!"

Some of the other Red Sox in the dugout were picking up on it now. They started yelling stuff out at the Dodger pitcher. Ben Porter called time and hurried out to the mound.

"Forget this guy," he said, pulling off his mask. "He's just a hot dog."

Magic looked up sharply. "No, he's not."

"Sure, he is."

The catcher looked in toward the Dodger dugout. He was getting a signal from the bench.

"Look," he said, handing Magic the ball. "Brush this guy back, okay? That'll cool his jets."

"Brush him back?"

"Yeah. High and tight. Give him a shave."

Magic was shaking his head. "I can't do that," he said. "I might hit him."

"Aw, you won't hit him. He'll get out of the way."

"And if he doesn't?"

Porter thought for a moment. "It'll help his big mouth."

But Magic still refused. The catcher was putting his mask back on.

"Look, kid. You've got to do it. Orders from the high command, you know what I mean?"

Porter went back and squatted behind the plate. As Magic went into his windup, the picture flashed into his mind of the time he had beaned the batter back in Orlando. Like a movie running fast forward in his brain, he saw all the wild pitches he had thrown since then. He saw the ball skipping and hopping all over the place, and he saw batters diving and twisting to get out of the way.

Magic kicked and fired. The ball did just what the doctor ordered. It sailed in toward the waiting batter like a slow breaking ball. Except it didn't break. It stayed up and in. It was headed right for Green's head.

At the last second, Green jerked backward and fell to the dirt. The catcher lunged up to his left and caught the ball.

Up on the mound, Magic let out a huge sigh of relief. He didn't even want to begin to think what would have happened if he had beaned his own friend. Magic got the ball back from the catcher.

He looked back in to the plate. To his surprise, Green was already up and back in the box. Green had a huge smile on his face as he stood and waited. His bat was weaving just over his shoulder. Porter called for the split-fingered fastball. But as Magic went into his motion, he had the feeling that he could throw a B-B right now, *half* a B-B, and old DT would still get a good piece of it.

Magic delivered the pitch, and Green jumped all over it. Magic spun around and watched as the ball sailed out over right field, right over the row of palm trees behind the fence. Home run. A pair of "ones" flashed up on the scoreboard. One hit. One run. So much for that.

Green rounded the bases without making a big show of it, even though the crowd was on its feet, screaming. Of course he felt fantastic about the homer, but he decided to play it cool this time.

Coach Brooks had sent him up there to do some damage to the no-hitter, and he had sure done just that.

The Sox were on their feet as Green got back to the dugout. They mobbed him. They grabbed his cap off his head and beat him on the back. Hands flew up in the air to high-five him.

Out in the stands, the crowd had started to chant.

"Green! Green! Green!"

Green made his way through the players to the water cooler. Coach Brooks was standing there.

"Nice hit, Green," he said. That's all. Nice hit.

"Thanks," Green mumbled as he got a drink of water. The crowd was still chanting, and they were pounding their feet on the stands.

"Green! Green! Green!"

Coach Brooks looked at his player. "Aren't you going to take a curtain call?"

Green felt himself turning red. "Uh . . . nah. I don't think so."

Brooks leaned his head out of the dugout and looked up at the crowd.

"It's up to you, Green" he said. "But personally, I think you're nuts. I'd go for it."

Green couldn't believe his ears. "You would?"

The coach shrugged. A tiny grin was on his face. "Sure. Why not? It was a good hit."

In a flash, Green was out of the dugout. The crowd roared. Green raised his arms and acknowledged the crowd. In the dugout, Coach Brooks took off his cap.

"Green!" he called out. "Catch!"

Brooks flipped the hat out to Green. Green caught it, and waved it in the air. The crowd roared again. They even started stamping their feet.

TWELVE

Magic was waiting outside the players' entrance when Cake Man Green came strolling out with some of the other players.

"Uh-oh," said Peter Kenney, hiding a smile. "Looks like the president of the 'thanks for ruining my no hitter, you creep' fan club. I wonder if he wants your autograph."

Green introduced Magic to his teammates.

"We've met," Kenney joked. "I was the guy out there today who was striking out to make you look good."

"You're real polite in these parts."

Kenney shrugged. "Hey, anything we can do . . ." Green and Magic split up from the others.

"What's wrong?" Kenney joked. "You don't want to bore us about how great you guys were back in high school?"

Green punched him in the arm. "Yeah. Something like that."

As soon as the others had left, Green turned to his friend. A serious look had come over his face.

"Magic, I'm sorry about ruining your no-hitter. I just—"

Magic cut him off. "Hey, the ball hung a little and you creamed it. That's just the way it goes."

"It didn't hang!" Green shot back. "That was your killer pitch. I creamed it!"

Magic laughed. "You sure did. And now I'm going to cream you!"

Magic dropped down into a wrestler's stance, like the fake wrestlers on TV. So did Green. The two circled each other, making faces and growling and clawing their hands in the air.

"You're history, Green." Magic snarled.

"What do you know about history? You flunked it."

"I wouldn't talk."

"I wish you wouldn't!"

They charged in and locked arms and grappled for about a minute. They were both laughing so hard that it was pretty lame wrestling, and they finally pulled apart.

"But seriously," Green said as the two caught their breath, "you were really awesome out there. I don't think I've ever seen a guy so pumped up."

Magic laughed. "Are you forgetting a certain 'chew them up and spit them out' second baseman we both know?"

Green made a face. "Oh, well, Scrapper, sure.

But Scrap gets pumped up just pouring milk on his cereal in the morning."

They both laughed. But they also both knew it was true. Nobody could beat their friend when it came to energy. Nobody. They couldn't wait to see him.

As it turned out, they didn't have long to wait. Green and Magic went off for some fried chicken, and while they were eating it, a bus passed by on the street. Magic looked up and saw it.

"Scrapper!" he yelled.

Green looked up. The bus said White Sox on the side.

"Let's go!" Green cried.

The two of them bolted out of the fast-food stand without even finishing their meal. They raced down the sidewalk as the bus rounded a corner up ahead.

"Come on!" Green called out. "I know a short-cut!"

He took a sudden right, and cut down a small side street that ran through a neighborhood. Magic followed. They zigzagged through the neighborhood, and came out at a 7–11. The motel where the White Sox would be staying was right across the street. The bus was just pulling into the driveway.

"Wait!" Magic called out. Green pulled up. "Hold on," Magic said. "I'll be right back."

He ran into the 7–11. Green could see him buying something at the counter.

"What did you get?" he asked when Magic came back outside.

"Just hold on. You'll see."

The two dashed across the street. They stationed themselves just off to the side of the bus.

"Here," Magic said, pulling something from his pocket. Green looked and saw what it was.

"Perfect!"

A couple minutes later, when Scrapper came down off the bus, he heard two *very* familiar voices talking.

"I'll trade you one Magic Ramirez for a Cake Man Green."

"Sure. That's cool. I'll do that."

"How about a Glen Mitchell? You got anything to trade for a Mitchell?"

"Are you kidding? Him? I've got a bunch of Mitchells I can't get rid of."

Green and Magic were standing off to the side, swapping baseball cards. Scrapper dropped his travel bag on the ground and sauntered over to them like a cowboy who had been on his horse too long.

"Well, you guys want them autographed?" he said.

Green and Magic looked up at him and frowned. "You can't write?" Green said.

Scrapper just shook his head and chuckled. "Laurel and Hardy, I swear."

That was it for the jokes. Scrapper held out his hands and the other two slapped him a pound of skin. Immediately the three of them started talking all at once. They were going a mile a minute, trying to cram all that had happened in the last month and a half into the next five minutes. When they suddenly realized what they were doing, they burst out laughing.

"Wait here," Scrapper said. "I'll be back in five minutes."

"Hey," Green said, "we're important people. Make it three."

Scrapper took his bag up to his room, then met the other two back outside.

"Have you guys had dinner?" he asked. Green and Magic looked at each other and suddenly remembered the chicken they had left on the table.

"We know where you can get some fried chicken," Green said. "Cheap." He and Magic burst out laughing. Scrapper just shook his head.

"You guys are sick."

They went back to a nearby pizza joint and sat there telling stories about these last months down in Florida. Green told how Coach Brooks had been riding him all spring.

"But your stats are great," Scrapper said. "I've been keeping an eye on you in the newspaper. Why would he climb on you? Nobody's ever climbed on you."

"Yeah, I know," Green said. "But I think that's just it. We're not talking high school anymore, we're talking major leagues. Back then it was like I could do no wrong. But what's a high-school hero to a bunch of professional ballplayers?"

Magic was nodding his head. "Yeah, it's been a lot tougher than we thought, hasn't it?"

They all agreed on that. A *lot* tougher.

"Okay," said Green, as he finished up his pizza. "Let's have the scoop now. Which one of us hotshots is going to be there on Opening Day?" He looked around the table as no one said a word. "Don't all start talking at once," he said.

"You and I've got one more game to play," Scrapper reminded him.

"I know. But the way I see it, my team's roster has pretty much shaped up. And there's just no room for me on it. I mean, how many guys can you cram into center field?"

"You don't think you're going to make it?" Magic asked.

"I get this feeling that the coach would just as soon trade me away to another team. I don't know."

"How about Triple A?" Magic asked.

"Sure. Triple A would be fine. I mean, I'd still be with the team. I really want to play for Boston."

"Aw, you'll make it," Magic said. "I can feel it."

Green laughed. "Uh-oh. The famous Ramirez vibes."

He turned to Scrapper, who wasn't saying anything.

"How about you, Scrap? Are you going to be this season's Rookie of the Year?"

Scrapper looked up from his pizza. "Shoe Salesman of the Year is more like it."

Magic let out a cry. "What is this? I thought *I* was supposed to be the downer around here."

"Yeah, Scrap?" Green said. "What's up?"

Scrapper took a deep breath and then told them

all about his father's surprise visit and about being booted from the game. He told them about his slump.

"You'll snap out of it," Green said.

"When?" Scrapper snapped. "The last game is tomorrow, in case you forgot."

"Well, what has your father said about your slump?" Magic asked. "He's been through everything. What does he suggest?"

Scrapper looked up sharply. "What does he say? Are you kidding? I haven't even told him."

"You haven't?"

"No way! I haven't talked to him since he left." Magic couldn't believe it.

"Scrap! He's your dad! What do you mean, you haven't talked to him?"

Scrapper shrugged. "It's my slump, not his," he mumbled.

"But we always used to go to your dad for advice," Green said. "I can't believe you haven't talked to him, Scrap. Boy, I'd have been on the phone in a second if . . ."

Scrapper didn't say anything, so Green and Magic dropped the subject. They finished their pizzas and took off. The sun had started to go down. The horizon was a wild mix of orange and blue.

The three friends strolled along in no particular direction. In no time, they found themselves standing outside the empty ball park. They looked at each other and slowly a big smile grew on their faces. It was Scrapper who spoke first.

"Pla-a-y ball!"

Ten minutes later, Magic Ramirez stood on the mound, flipping the ball around in his hand. Cake Man Green stood at the plate, digging in. All that was missing was a fielder.

Scrapper came running out onto the field.

Scrapper ran out to the infield. He banged his fist into his glove and got up on his toes. He was psyched.

"Hey batter, batter! Come on, Magic. This guy's got no eye. My mother can hit better than him. Blow it past him. Hey, batter, batter . . ."

THIRTEEN

It was another perfect day for baseball. The stands were packed. Out in the bleachers, some people were rubbing on suntan lotion.

Magic decided to sit behind home plate. He didn't want to choose sides. Suddenly, somebody bumped into him from behind.

"Hey, watch your—Coach La Russo!" Roberts shouted.

"Thought I'd surprise you boys. Hell, I needed a little sun, anyway. I flew down with Joe Mitchell."

"I can't believe it! The other guys will flip out!"

Coach La Russo settled in his seat.

"This is a first," he said. "I get to cheer for both teams."

The crowd let out a huge cheer as the Red Sox took the field. The lineups were announced over the PA system. Magic and La Russo didn't relax until they heard that both Green and Scrapper were in the starting lineup.

"They'd better be playing," La Russo joked. "I didn't come all the way down here just to watch the palm trees."

Because it was the last game of spring training, television crews from Chicago and Boston were on hand. It felt almost like Opening Day. Magic looked up into the press box and saw Ted Leonard sitting there, the guy from ABC-TV in Chicago.

As the game commenced, Magic kept up a running chatter, giving his former coach the book on each of the players.

"This one chases them wide every time."

"Dynamite arm, Coach. Bionic."

"Ready for a sinker . . . ? What did I tell you?"

La Russo was impressed. It was hard to believe that only two years ago the young pitcher sitting next to him was just another student at Rosemont High. The coach sat and listened as his former player rattled off the stats on these major-league players like it was the most natural thing in the world.

"Okay, here's a guy I want to know about," La Russo said as a certain number seven for the Red Sox stepped up to bat.

Magic laughed. "This guy? His name's Green. Thinks he's hot stuff. He's okay, I guess."

"What's his favorite pitch?" La Russo asked.

Magic laughed again. "Any pitch."

And Green proved it. The next pitch in was a shoulder-high fastball. Green rapped it into shallow left for a single. He got to the bag, then took a decent lead as the next batter stepped in.

"Look!" Magic said, pointing out toward second base. La Russo looked.

Scrapper was edging in toward the bag. He beat his fist into his glove and kept glancing over at first base.

"He's got a hunch," La Russo said.

Magic answered, "I think it's a good one."

On the very next pitch, Green took off. He got a good jump on the ball. The throw from the catcher was high, and Scrapper had to leap into the air to pull it down. Green slid in under him. He was safe.

Green called time and he got up and dusted himself off.

"Well, fancy meeting you here," he said to Scrapper.

"Yeah," Scrapper said. "I was just on my way to the major leagues and I thought I'd stop off for a visit."

"That so?"

Scrapper tugged at his cap and leaned forward for the next pitch. "Hope so," he said.

The pitcher set and fired. The batter swung.

Crack!

It was a bouncing ball toward the gap between first and second. As Scrapper dove for the ball, Green took off for third. Scrapper got the ball on the bounce and fell to the dirt. He scrambled to his feet and made a move to third. But Green had too good a jump. Scrapper turned and fired to first for the out.

Up in the stands, Coach La Russo turned to Magic.

"Do you think Scrap let him go?"

"Coach, we're talking about *Scrapper* here, remember?"

La Russo laughed. "Right. I forgot."

At the plate the next inning, Scrapper slapped the ball into the left-field corner. He raced around first and made it to second standing up. The next batter sent a bouncer into center field. By the time Green had gloved the ball, Scrapper was already tearing around third. The coach was waving him home.

Green uncorked a rocket. The ball flashed past the cutoff man and got to the plate on one hop. The catcher had just enough time to catch the ball and make a half-turn before Scrapper came barreling into him. The two went flying in a cloud of dust. The crowd leaped to their feet.

The umpire was right on top of the play. When the dust cleared, the catcher was on his back, staring up at the sky. Scrapper was on his back, too, one arm stretched out over the plate. The umpire turned around and saw the ball still rolling back toward the fence. He swept his arms in front of him.

"Safe!

From where he was, still on his back, Scrapper thrust two fists into the air.

"All right!" he yelled. Scrapper jumped to his

feet and pumped his fists in the air. When he got back to the dugout, he was mobbed.

In the middle innings, the game blew completely open. The White Sox scored four in the sixth and two more in the seventh. Scrapper contributed again, with a broken-bat single and a stolen base.

But the Red Sox battled right back. They got three of the runs back in the eighth. Going into the ninth, it was the White Sox 7–6.

As Green stood out in center field in the top of the ninth he caught himself thinking about that first day of spring training. It seemed like a hundred years ago. He turned around and looked at the palm trees running along the back fence. For just a second, he had actually expected to see that they had grown taller.

Come on, he said to himself, laughing. *Spring training has been long, but it hasn't been* that *long!*

The next thing Green knew, he was on a dead run toward the infield. If someone would have asked him, he'd have said that he never even saw the pitch, let alone heard the crack of the bat. His body just automatically reacted. The ball was a weakly hit blooper over second base. Green's legs moved like pistons. At the last second, he lunged and stretched out his glove. The ball dropped into it just as the big center fielder hit the ground. He tumbled over several times, but kept hold of the ball.

It was only when Green looked up to see the runner slowing down around second base that he even realized who he had robbed him of a hit. It was Scrapper.

The White Sox remained scoreless for the rest of the inning. Boston was still behind by one. The first Red Sox batter in the bottom of the ninth drew a walk. The pitcher was pulled. The reliever put the next two batters down in order. The crowd had suddenly gone silent. One more out and spring season was over.

Cake Man Green was up next. Coach Brooks went up to him as he headed out of the dugout. He touched his elbow and tugged on his ear.

"You know that this means Green?"

Green was stunned. "Sure. It means bunt."

Brooks cut him off. "Right. Don't do it."

Green gave his coach a quick smile. "Got it."

As David stepped into the batter's box he looked back at the crowd behind the plate. Something there caught his eye. It was Coach La Russo, standing up. He was urgently tapping his left hand on his right shoulder.

Green turned back around and faced the pitcher. His mind was reeling. *Left hand, right shoulder.* It was one of the coach's old signals. But which one was it? Green couldn't remember.

The ball came in letter high. Green's bat didn't leave his shoulder.

"Strike!"

Green took the next two pitches for balls, then fouled off the next one. He was still racking his brain to try to figure out the signal. The next pitch came in high, and Green held off from it.

Three balls, two strikes. Full count.

Green stepped out of the batter's box and adjusted his glove. He looked up into the stands again, but now everyone was on their feet. He couldn't spot La Russo.

Left hand, right shoulder.

"Come on, Green! Good eye, good eye!"

Green looked back at the dugout. Coach Brooks was up on the top step, leading the pepper. Green couldn't believe it.

"Let's go now!" Brooks called out. "Wait for your pitch! Stay loose!"

Suddenly Green remembered what La Russo's signal meant. Whenever Green tensed up, his right shoulder had a tendency to tighten up. It made his swing awkward. Left hand to right shoulder was La Russo's old signal to remind him. It simply meant, relax, stay loose.

Green stepped back into the box and took a few lazy swings. The catcher was saying something to him, but the crowd was so loud that Green couldn't even hear him. He looked out at the row of palm trees behind the outfield fence. They were perfectly still. No wind. If he was going to land one out there, it would have to be all on his own.

"Knee high," Green muttered, swinging the bat one more time. He squinted out at the pitcher. "Just one sweet pitch." The pitcher got his sign. He went into his windup and delivered a blazing fast ball . . . knee high.

Green swung.

FOURTEEN

The Red Sox locker room was like a party. Green's dramatic ninth-inning home run had been the perfect capper for the spring season. The players were flapping towels at each other and throwing stuff around. The pressure was finally off, at least for now.

Green was sitting in front of his locker. Pete Kenney came over to him and slapped him on the back.

"Well, Shorty. Not a bad spring, if I do say so myself."

"I sure like the way it ended," Green said.

"Yeah," Kenney said, laughing. "What's the big idea, anyway, showing off like that? Are you trying to make the rest of us look bad?"

Green pulled off his shoes and tossed them into the locker. "Now you sound like Brooks," he said.

Just then the coach appeared from around the corner.

"Did someone say my name?" Brooks asked. Green felt his face turning red. The coach continued. "Green, as soon as you're dressed, see me in my office."

The rookie center fielder nodded his head. "Okay."

Brooks moved off.

"Well, that's it," Green said to Kenney as soon as Brooks was out of earshot. "That didn't sound much like 'welcome to the team' to me."

"Are you kidding?" Kenney said. "You just hit the game-winning hit. They're not going to drop you now."

Green wasn't so sure. "I've got a hunch they're going to trade me."

"Where?"

"I don't know. To somebody's farm team. They just don't need any more hitters on this team."

"Do you really think they'd trade you?"

Green shrugged. "I guess we'll see."

Kenney headed off for the showers. Green sat there, staring at his jersey, which was hung up in the locker: Red Sox.

He thought about Fenway Park. About the Green Monster. What if he never got the chance to play in Boston after all this? It just didn't seem possible.

Green slammed his locker shut. He stood up and headed for Coach Brooks's office. He didn't even take the time to dry his hair or pack his bag.

He just couldn't wait any longer. Brooks was at his desk when Green walked in.

"Well, kind of anxious, aren't you?" Brooks said.

"I guess I don't like to wait around for bad news," Green said.

"And you think I've got bad news for you?"

"I don't know."

Brooks came around and leaned against the front of his desk.

"You like this team, don't you, Green?" he asked.

Green nodded. "Sure."

"But you know, we've already got a lot of good hitters."

Here is comes, Green thought. "Yes," he said. "I know that."

The coach crossed his arms. "I guess you think I've been riding you pretty hard all spring," he said. "And maybe I have. But that's my job, Green. I've got to make sure that when we bring you up onto the team that you're ready mentally as well as physically."

Green wasn't sure he had just heard correctly.

"Did you say 'when'?"

"Sure. We just don't have room for you now. You'll go to our Triple A club in Providence next week. It's close to Boston. We can keep an eye on you. Then, once the season gets under way, who knows—"

Green cut him off.

"I made the team?" he cried.

Coach Brooks chuckled. "Well, sure, you made the team. Did you ever doubt it?"

Green was stunned. Coach Brooks stepped forward and shook his hand.

"Welcome to the team."

Out in the locker room, Kenney and a few of the other players grinned as they heard a gigantic "*Ya-hoo!*" coming from Coach Brooks's office.

Magic and Coach La Russo were out in the parking lot tossing a ball back and forth when Green came running out of the ball park.

"Triple A!" he cried out. "Another month or so and I ought to be safely inside Fenway Park! They're keeping me!"

Magic ran up to him and gave him a high-five.

"Excellent! I knew you'd make it!"

"Those famous Ramirez vibes!"

Coach La Russo came over and shook his hand.

"Congratulations, Dave. I'm proud of you."

Green couldn't stop smiling. He was about to say something, but just then Scrapper came bursting out of the ball park. He was griping like an old lady.

"They're nuts. They don't know what they're doing. It's ridiculous!"

"What wrong?" Green joked. "Are you sore over the hit I robbed from you?"

Scrapper had his glove with him. He threw it at Green.

"Who cares about a little hit?"

"Hey, so what's the deal?" Magic asked.

"I'll tell you the deal!" Scrapper exploded. "The deal is, they won't put me on the team! They're shipping me off the Triple A! Can you believe it?"

Magic and Green and La Russo couldn't help themselves. They broke out laughing. Scrapper looked at them like they were all crazy.

"What's so funny?" he snapped. "I'm booted off the team and you guys are laughing."

Coach La Russo was the first to stop laughing enough to talk. He put his arm around his former player.

"You never let up, do you, Scrap?" he said.

"What do you mean?" Scrapper asked suspiciously.

"Green here has just been told that he made Triple A and he's ten feet off the ground. You get told the same thing and you're ready to kill someone."

Scrapper turned to Green. "Triple A? You?"

Green nodded. "Yep."

"And you're *happy* about it?"

"Well, it would have been great to go straight to Boston, sure. But come on, Scrap. Triple A is as close as you get without actually being there."

"But I want to *be* there."

"It's just a matter of time," Coach La Russo said.

Scrapper looked at him. "Do you think so?"

"Let me ask you this," the coach said. "When the Phillies signed your dad, where did he play his first season?"

Scrapper thought for a second.

"Triple A!" he cried. Now Scrapper was psyched. "All right! We'll tear that league up! No problem! They'd better watch out!"

He stopped suddenly and turned to Ramirez.

"Wait a minute. What about you, Magic? I'm so busy crabbing about me, I didn't even ask you. What are you doing?"

"Well," said Magic. "They gave me the word about Triple A yesterday right after the game."

"You mean when we were playing ball together last night you already *knew*?"

"Yep."

"Why didn't you tell us?" Green asked.

"I didn't want to jinx you."

Green and Scrapper started to beat up on their friend.

"So, what's the word, Mr. Jinx?" Scrapper asked after they got up. "Good or bad?"

"Bad for you, sucker," Magic answered. "Our first game is against *you*!"

There were high-fives all around. Even Coach La Russo. Magic and Green and Scrapper looked at each other as it finally began to sink in just how far along they had gotten. More than ever, it just seemed like a matter of time before they made it into the major league. Maybe months. Maybe weeks!

Magic hit Scrapper on the arm. "And you were going to sell shoes!"

"Hey, look," Green said suddenly.

Ted Leonard was coming across the parking lot toward them. The minicam crew was right behind him.

"Hi, guys," Leonard said when he got up to them. "Hey, this is great. I've got you all together." Then he spotted La Russo. "Coach! You, too? Great! How about a group interview? What do you say? Something for the poor folks back in snowy Chicago."

"It's snowy back home?" Magic asked.

"Ten inches last night."

The cameraman flipped on his light. The sound man handed Leonard the microphone.

"You ready?" Leonard said.

"Wait," Scrapper said. He and the others turned away for a second. Leonard couldn't see what they were doing. When they turned back around, all three of them were wearing sunglasses. They bunched together and looked up at the camera.

"Yeah, we're ready."

Follow our ROOKIES when the big call comes and they get set to burn up the majors in:

ROOKIES #4: BIG-LEAGUE BREAK